WALKING

UNDER

His

WINGS

WALKING

UNDER

His

WINGS

GOD PERFECT KEYS FOR
A BLESSED AND FRUITFUL LIFE

EFRAIN A. SANCHEZ-RIVERA, MD

XULON PRESS

Xulon Press
2301 Lucien Way #415
Maitland, FL 32751
407.339.4217
www.xulonpress.com

Unless otherwise indicated, Scripture quotations taken from the Holman Christian Standard Bible (HCSB). Copyright © 1999, 2000, 2002, 2003, 2009 by Holman Bible Publishers, Nashville Tennessee. All rights reserved.

Scripture quotations taken from the King James Version (KJV) – *public domain.*

Paperback ISBN-13: 978-1-6312-9873-8
Ebook ISBN-13: 978-1-6312-9874-5

I dedicate this project first to my God,
my rock and deliverer, who has always
protected and sheltered my life.

Also, to my lovely wife Aixa,
who has always loved and supported me,
along with my children, Efrain and Ainesis,
my inspiration and my pearls from heaven.

I love you all to the moon and back.

TABLE OF CONTENTS

Prologue
THE BEGINNING

Humankind has been confined to this beautiful and remarkable place we named Earth to endure their lives until they're called into the Lord's presence. First and foremost, we are here because our Creator made us and put His own breath into our bodies to grant us life. After Adam's and Eve's first encounter with evil and their subsequent fall, the couple was expelled from the Garden of Eden into the unknown to earn their living through hard work and survive the best way they could until redemption was delivered.

Living in this world, we are in front of a large crowd of witnesses, both good and evil, and every action, step, or breath we take is potentially influenced by supernatural forces. On every individual's journey, he or she will be affected by heavenly creatures and, at times, evil ones. Our experiences and what we learn from them will help us seek the real path throughout our lives and find the answers to all our questions.

Our path will be intersected by angelic entities sent from the heavens with a mission to protect and guard us, and even to help us reach our prophetic destiny. The Lord desires that we all seek His face and open our hearts to let Him in as our Redeemer and Savior. Every journey is different, but the challenges, struggles, fears, and victories are extremely similar in each life. We need to prepare ourselves and keep our senses on alert to be able to hear the voice of God calling each one of us to walk under His wings.

Chapter One
THE FIRST SCREAM

The sky started to brighten with the colorful rays of the morning dawn. The night was incredibly quiet and quite peaceful for most of the people. As the golden master star of the sky saluted the earth with its warmth and brightness, the city started to awaken and begin its usual rituals. The day started routinely, like any other. Same routine, same duties, same steps to fulfill before going on with the day. At least that was the way it seemed for everyone in the Rivers household. Not for Edward, though. Unfortunately for him, his first-morning memory was still fuzzy. Having that kind of feeling really frustrated him since he hated to feel he didn't have control of something. All his life, he had learned to be in control and to avoid letting his goals be derailed. That was a hard expectation for an eleven-year-old, but that was always expected from him. Because of that situation, sometimes he felt out of place, different from everyone else. He was tall for his age, a little heavier than any youngster would like to be, with hair as dark as onyx and expressive brown eyes. He was very clumsy and didn't do well in sports, but he enjoyed reading, investigating, and submerging in a world of awe and wonders.

Edward was still trying to remember what exactly had happened that morning around four thirty. He recalled a scream inside the bedroom he shared with his little brother, Anthony, but wasn't sure who or what it was. He opened his eyes suddenly when he heard that guttural, eerie sound. His next memory was him stumbling out of bed, dropping his bedside lamp, falling to the floor three times, and ultimately arriving at the bathroom, where he dropped a glass, which broke into zillion pieces. He knew something was not right. He was never this clumsy. Luckily for him, his parents didn't get up at that time, and he was able to quickly clean up the bathroom mess. The family had to go on with all their morning routine, and Edward couldn't invest too much time deciphering the mystery. Before he knew it, he was already in his mother's car heading to his grandmother's house, the first stop before heading to school.

During the trip toward his grandmother's house, Edward's mind started to fly into the clouds. He remembered the events he considered crucial and influential in his life. Being the son of two well-respected public schoolteachers in town had been a significant burden on the shoulders of a preteen child. Sometimes it was too much to handle. He was raised to be the perfect son, the ideal student, the model child, nothing less. Unfortunately, the load of that imposition was taking a toll on his life. Loneliness, rejection, bullying, and sadness were just some of the many bitter experiences he'd had to endure. All that had made him extremely dedicated to his books and dreams; and to his classmates, an arrogant know-it-all. He was just an average, nerdy, shy, sentimental youngster. All those features had made him very introverted—and, lately, very submerged in a different world.

"Edward, are you all right, dear?" said his mom, worried. "I know you're distracted most of the time, but today you seem very distant. Are you feeling sick?"

"No, Mom, I'm fine. Just a little tired. I didn't sleep well last night."

"No wonder. You're involved in so many meetings and activities lately. With your schoolwork load, I'm afraid it's becoming a burden on you. You may need to cut back some of it."

"No, Mom, it's okay. It's not that. Being in those groups is fun for me, and I'm doing all right in my classes. I really need to do this. Please don't pull me out of those activities." Edward's plea came from the deepest part of his being.

Wendy Rivers felt some remorse for asking her son to cut back on his activities. How could she ask that from him if that was precisely what she filled her days with? Regarded as one of the best first-grade teachers in the district, she also volunteered as coordinator for all the graduations and dramas for the entire school. She was often called upon to use her talent to organize dramatic presentations at other schools. Now Edward was following a similar path. Unfortunately, she also noted that despite his facade, her son's journey was lonely and painful, very similar to the one she had taken when she was his age.

But not everything seemed gloomy and catastrophic for Edward. During his times alone in "his" world, he had started to talk to someone who appeared to be listening to him. He would share his deepest thoughts and concerns, and he swore he could almost feel a voice deep within him, answering back. As time went by, the youngster began to realize that the person listening was indeed God Himself. He did not want to share this newfound insight with anyone just yet, fearing he might be considered crazy or a fanatic. Edward felt a profound and pleasant peace every time he was able to share his thoughts and concerns with Him. He always knew that something extraordinary would come back as a response. He had no idea that all these interactions were part of spiritual training that the Heavenly Father had initiated through the Holy Spirit's intervention in preparation for the years to come.

The night was still and quiet. The silence dominating most of the evening was almost deafening. Everything seemed promising and ideal to the untrained eye, but for the two angelic creatures guarding the Rivers household, that was just a facade. The two heavenly entities were enormous—just short of ten feet tall—majestic, and beautiful. They were both wearing what seemed to be golden tunics over a shiny ivory armor fastened at the waist with a golden belt, and they were armed with fire swords. They knew a battle was blooming on the horizon, although they were not yet clear about why they'd been sent to this location. The Rivers family was not even involved in any specific ministry, but the angels had learned a long time ago not to question God's instructions. They just obeyed and stayed on guard, ready to execute any new directives as they were delivered by their Creator. As created beings, they were aware of the scripture that stated that we are all in front of a big crowd of witnesses,[1] which includes humans and angels, but also demonic entities.

"I don't like this at all," one angel said. "It seems quiet, but something terrible is about to happen."

"Yes, indeed," the other angel said. "I can feel a storm brewing already. It will explode any minute. I only wonder, why them? They're only kids. Why is the old guardian cherub[2] interested in attacking humans that have done nothing to him?"

"It is his nature," said the first. "Remember that once he fell with his followers and tricked Adam and Eve into sinning in the garden of Eden, he was granted permission to rule over the earth. That includes attempts to harm, manipulate, use, and even control human beings. The difference is that once men recognize God's authority over their lives, salvation and grace will enact. That allows the Holy Spirit to come in and transform, counsel, heal, and protect their souls from these attacks." And that was undoubtedly a wonderful promise and hope for eternity.

Shortly after three in the morning, the entire environment suddenly changed, becoming so oppressively heavy it was almost impossible to stand. The nocturnal silence was

---

[1] Hebrews 12:1. Holman Christian Standard Bible (HCSB). 2009. Holman Bible Publishers, Nashville TN.

[2] Ezekiel 28:14-16. Holman Christian Standard Bible (HCSB). 2009. Holman Bible Publishers. Nashville, TN.

interrupted by a novel, eerie, and terrifying sound. As the angels shifted their attention toward the noise, they immediately realized the scope of their mission. The scream, the first of its kind at this location, came from young Edward Rivers' spirit, manifested in the earthly realm as part of what is commonly called a seizure. The sound was meant that demonic figures were getting ready to attack the young man and cause complications. The angels immediately acted to protect Edward's surroundings. Simultaneously, they sensed how the Holy Spirit transmitted strength and life into the ailing youngster's spirit to help him endure the ongoing crisis.

The demons were trying to strangle Edward's spirit. Their appearance was horrifying. Initially hidden within the texture and drawings of the children's window curtains, they suddenly emerged as commanded, ready to attack. Their heads were similar to those of dragons — big, with fiery, red eyes. They had long, bony arms with big claws. Their torsos seemed human-like, but the skin was scaled and shiny at the same time, and their legs ended in goat-like hooves. Their voices were terrible and eerie, and they expressed their fury immediately upon seeing the presence of the two heavenly warriors.

One of the angels ran next to Anthony, and the other stronger one assisted Edward. Once the angels responded in the name of the Son of God, the demons were immediately weakened and unable to harm the young lad's spirit. Using their fire swords as needed, they were able to keep the monsters at bay while the Holy Ghost made His presence stronger and more definite.

The angelic beings were able to protect both children from any further attacks. That's when they realized their presence was commissioned in response to constant prayers from the young lads' mother and grandmothers. They were also amazed that Edward was able to get up immediately after the episode concluded, but he was still unable to control his body. The angels helped him reach the bathroom and clean up the glass he'd accidentally broke, and they kept his parents in bed. As the sun rose, the angels knew the struggle was not over; it was only beginning. Another crisis was brewing on the horizon, and this time it was going to be extreme.

Chapter Two

THE FIRST STORM

E dward allowed his mind to fly once more beyond the limits of the backseat of his mother's vehicle. He was still puzzled about the events from the early morning and wanted to ask his friend in heaven what that could be. Unfortunately, he always felt shy to do that when other people were close by, even his parents. Being timid and reserved about everything, Edward had no real friends, just acquaintances. He participated in some athletic activities to please his father, but in reality, he was happy with his books, his world, and his conversations with God.

Edward was feeling strange and uneasy that morning. It was so difficult for him to explain it since he'd never felt this way before. He chose to keep silent, since his desire was to go to school. It was his only real escape, and expressing that openly made him feel all right. "I'm glad the annual field day carnival is coming up soon," he thought. I guess I'm just overwhelmed with the end-of-year activities. However, the statement was not enough to relieve his internal fear. Deep inside him, something was very shaky, unstable, edgy. Something extreme was about to happen, he was sure. But what? Only time would produce an answer.

The time spent at his grandmother's house seemed an endless routine. At least, that was the case in the eyes of everyone there, all except for Nana. Edward's grandmother was the matriarch of the entire clan. She was a very stoic and strong lady in her late sixties who had worked on a farm her whole life. Nana always knew when something was not right with her grandkids. The main reason for this was that she was the one who'd raised them. She often fashioned her hair in a small bow on the back of her head. The hairstyle always looked beautiful, even though it was starting to be adorned with salt and pepper touches.

As soon as Nana received Edward into her arms for their morning embrace, she instantly perceived that something was definitely out of balance. "Oh dear, what is wrong, Edward?" she asked gently. "Something's troubling you. Are you getting sick?"

Edward hesitated for a moment. "No, ma'am, I'm fine," he finally said in his most polite manner.

"I asked him the same thing on our way over here," his mother, Wendy, said. "But he said he just didn't sleep well."

"How about that? Well, it's Thursday, and tomorrow is a teachers-only workday, so you'll have time to rest after school is over today," Nana finally said, closing the discussion.

Not for him, though. School finals, the Juvenile Credit Union Officers' annual convention, and mandatory meetings for his sixth-grade graduation were all organizing on the horizon. They seemed like predestined missiles ready to launch. No, he needed to take advantage of every second to complete all his duties in a timely manner. Then maybe, just maybe, he would be able to relax a bit. He needed to find some time to talk to his celestial friend. God had priority over all the other activities and duties. He was the only reason Edward was able to go on.

Edward went to the bathroom before heading to school, and as soon the door closed, he opened his heart to his Creator. "Oh God, I don't know what's going on. I feel a burden inside, a deep sorrow that I can't comprehend. I know something is wrong, but I cannot decipher what it is!" He closed his eyes, and tears started to flow down his cheeks.

Abruptly, for the first time ever, he heard a voice inside his heart. "Do not be afraid. Trust Me. I will carry you on." The words came to him as a surprise, and Edward felt a sweet, sudden, fresh, profound, and yet inexplicable peace—a peace beyond understanding.[3] The feeling made him realize that regardless of any situation, God was in total control.

The short ride to the school was uneventful. Every single activity was conducted as usual—friends greeting friends, the school clowns making jokes about everything and everyone indiscriminately, the school official gossips at their corner creating their new stories, and so on. Everyone throughout the entire school was busy as bees in their beehive, all engaged in their skilled activities. Edward went straight to his American history classroom, which was the first period of the day. Mr. O'Reilly was already waiting at his desk. He was a war veteran, and he stood and walked around like he was about to march into the battlefield once more.

The history teacher was a tall and slender man, with hair only on the sides and back of his lustrous, bald head. He had a very inquisitive, sometimes troubling look in his eyes that brought chills to all his students. The way he looked at people was, at times, so penetrating that it felt like a sword cutting deep into the bottom of the soul. "Good morning, Edward," Mr. O'Reilly said.

"Good morning, sir," said the boy.

That was their daily morning routine. The professor's voice was always monotonous, but that day, Edward also noted a deep touch of sadness. Perhaps it was because of the appearance of his left hand, inert, motionless, almost dead-looking. It was a constant reminder of his encounter with war and death, and prominent evidence of the loneliness in his own life. Suddenly the morning bell rang, and the learning race was about to begin.

---

[3] Philippians 4:7. Holman Christian Standard Bible (HCSB). 2009. Holman Bible Publishers. Nashville, TN.

Every student lined up and entered the classroom as orderly as preteens could. As soon as everyone reached their seats, it was time to stand for the pledge of allegiance. Edward loved that part of the morning routine. To him it was a way of rededicating his life and day to the Father in heaven. He felt sad for those who were careless about it, not even enunciating the words. He chose not to judge them, though. He hoped that one day, every soul would believe, and then all would be able to talk to his friend in the celestial mansions as well. Once the prayer was completed, everyone sat at their desks, while Mr. O'Reilly announced the schedule for their daily activities. Amid all that, Edward heard the scream once more.

The eerie, guttural sound was thunderous this time, invading the entire classroom. Elvis, Edward's front seat neighbor, suddenly turned toward him when the noise began. Edward watched Elvis' face, become paler and distressed with horror. "Oh, my gosh! Oh my gosh!" Elvis yelled.

Edward then realized where the scream was coming from. The horrible, excruciating, ululating, ghostly sound was coming from his own mouth. He tried to bring his hand up to cover it. However, instead he felt how every muscle of his body tightened and started to shake uncontrollably. And suddenly, he sunk into the abyss of unconsciousness.

The angels received an urgent message directly from the commander-in-chief of the celestial armies. The communication stated that the storm in Edward's life was about to emerge. Therefore, their presence was required to engage in a new battle. Both angelic creatures were aware that they couldn't question or refuse a direct command from Jesus, so they transported themselves directly to Edward's school. They arrived while the student body was entering their classrooms and positioned themselves to join in on the pledge of allegiance.

While the students recited the pledge, the two heavenly entities remained on alert, waiting for the attack to emerge. They situated themselves close to Edward, but they were on high alert, and they were ready to detect any demonic presence or approach. Suddenly, they heard an explosion. Instantly, they saw a gigantic, gargoyle-like creature that rose in front of Edward, ready to attack and suffocate his ailing spirit. Both angels felt the strength that only came from the prayers sent straight to the Father's throne by Edward's relatives. That force allowed them to counterattack, blocking any harmful influence in the name of Jesus. Edward then passed out, and the Holy Ghost carried his spirit while the crisis endured.

Everything seemed like a strange dream. Edward was able to hear every voice, scream, cry, and even strong words around him. Nevertheless, everything was rolling in front of his eyes like an old movie. He saw how Mr. O'Reilly carried his limp body in his own arms. At the same time, his friend Elvis was holding his head, the same way a brother would do, protecting him from any harm.

Next to Mr. O'Reilly was Mr. Ross, the science teacher. "I will go with you," he said. "Let's go to the hospital right now."

Edward saw how they laid his body in the front seat of Mr. O'Reilly's pickup truck. While Mr. Ross drove, he was watching the boy and holding his chin up.

Edward realized then that this was not an old movie. He felt a sweet and extraordinary presence next to him. The entity was so bright he could not identify any features, but he was sure it was the Holy Spirit. His heart filled up with God's promise once more: "Do not be afraid. Trust me. I will carry you on." That was precisely what He did. Edward opened his eyes then. One minute, he was about to sit at his school desk, and now he was on his way to the City Community Hospital Emergency Department. Despite the storm, he felt a profound peace, and he was no longer afraid.

Chapter Three

THE JUMP

The entire family was reunited at Mrs. Orell's house for the uncomfortable task of attending a wake. Mrs. Orell was the owner of the local grocery store. Everybody in the neighborhood knew and admired her and her family. Edward's community was several miles away from the city, and her grocery store adjacent to her residence was the only one around. The location, particularly with her as the owner, was an oasis, not just because of being there but because she was an absolute angel on earth. Sadly, cancer had taken over her health and vitality in only three months, and she was finally resting forever.

Edward heard that she was rejoicing, which seemed strange to him under the circumstances. This made him curious, and he started to ask some friends about it, and even better, he decided to read about it in the Bible. What he discovered was absolutely outstanding. Edward read about the celestial mansions that are reserved for those who recognize Jesus as their absolute Savior and Redeemer. He learned of a place where you will live forever, have no physical or spiritual pain, and where your body will be transformed. There were details he had a hard time understanding, but he was sure about something—Jesus was the only way to the Father.

Edward was very uncomfortable at wakes or anything that had to do with dead people. He was very fond of Mrs. Orell, just like everyone else in the community. Be that as it may, going to the wake was not exactly his idea of a good way to spend a Friday night. Luckily, the house was situated across the street from the community playground park. He told his parents he was going to the park to kill some time with the neighborhood kids.

The playground was not too big. There were two distinct oval areas for children of different ages. The one on the right was for smaller kids, and the one on the left, directly across the street from Mrs. Orell's house, was the one for older children. Each little oval arena contained a swing, monkey bars, and a slide, all made of metal, in sizes suitable for each age group. Edward and his friends played for a little while and then decided to jump onto the monkey bars. Despite the availability of rides, they grew more bored with each passing minute. That was when Jason came up with an unconventional (and apparently fascinating) idea. "What if instead of going down the slide the normal way, we use the side support beams?" he said. The idea seemed exciting, although somewhat scary, considering the slide was twelve feet tall.

Everyone agreed to the dare, so Edward had no choice. The young lad gave in to peer pressure and got in line; otherwise, he'd have been called a coward and a baby. The youngster was not afraid of heights but realized how risky it was to come down the proposed way. He watched how the other kids were doing it. They positioned themselves with a very tight grasp on top of the side beam and proceeded to slide down feet first, like a worm or some other slimy creature.

Finally, Edward's turn came. "God, help me endure this," prayed silently. "Don't let anything wrong happen." He got himself into the right position. As soon as he started to slide down, his body made an abrupt 180 degree move down, which brought him face up instead of looking at the ground. The sudden jerk caused him to loosen his arms and legs, and he started to fall.

The fall was quick, although it seemed to last forever. Twelve feet later, Edward found himself breathless, with empty lungs facing the sky from the ground, but alive. He suddenly stood up and had to take a deep gasp of air and initiated a prolonged coughing spell. Edward then realized that he had no broken bones or serious injuries. He looked at Mrs. Orell's house, and he saw his parents and other people rushing to him, horrified. At that precise moment, he abruptly woke up realizing he was dreaming, finding himself in his room, in his own bed.

It wasn't the first time he'd had the dream, reliving the dramatic experience that occurred at the playground. Sitting at his bed that morning, he started to remember the events that he had endured lately—the entire ordeal at school—the big seizure, they called it—and his trip to the hospital. Edward also remembered the look on his mother's face when she'd realized it was him lying in the hospital bed. This time it was not his brother, Anthony, who was always the sickly one. They were sent home after several hours, and a family friend helped to expedite an appointment with a specialist for the following day. His entire life had come to a halt. Edward was concerned about what would happen next, but he was evidently not afraid. The dream he'd just had was indeed something that happened to him several years ago. Miraculously, Edward had endured no harm after a twelve feet fall. Everyone that witnessed his fall immediately thought he was going to be killed by such an impact.

Before the events of that day, Edward had always been bothered by that dream. He used to wake up in a cold sweat, anxious and in distress, but not this time. He felt a profound peace now. The dream had ended up differently. Edward usually woke up when he started to fall, amid the panic. However, this time, he had fallen, stood up, and realized he was unharmed. That soothed and comforted him, unlike his experience at other times, he fell asleep again, submerging himself into a different kind of dream.

The house was surrounded by a multitude of witnesses. Every instance a wake was celebrated, that opened the opportunity for angelic and demonic beings to roam around. The extension of that occurrence depended on the events that surrounded the individual person's demise. Edward was attending Mrs. Orell's wake with his family. As soon as he'd decided to wander into the community park, his guardian angel was activated. Edward's guardian angel was very tall, surrounded by a luminous aura. He was wearing a long, white, one-piece tunic with a bright golden belt.

Everything seemed to be under control. The children were having fun while the adults attended the event. However, the angelic being remembered the scripture that stated that the devil was always wandering like a roaring lion, looking for prey to eat.[4] Precisely then, he saw a small gargoyle, suggesting ominous ideas in some of the children's minds. The angel moved rather quickly when he spotted the demon. The evil entity was rebuked in the name of Jesus, and it had to flee. Unfortunately, a devious idea had already been planted in Jason's mind, and all the kids agreed on the fruitless adventure.

Edward's guardian angel noted that some of his companions were there to protect their assigned children. That gave him some relief, since they could probably join forces if needed. Nevertheless, the celestial being realized soon enough that the primary attack was going to be against Edward. He positioned himself close to Edward, hoping he would change his mind and decide not to follow the fatal advice given by Jason. However, he could not force him, since he had made the decision of his own free will. The curse of peer pressure had done it again, and Edward started to position himself on the side beam.

As soon as the guardian saw Edward falling, he immediately flew to the ground under him. He didn't know how he was going to handle the situation with all the human witnesses who

---

[4] 1 Peter 5:8. Holman Christian Standard Bible (HCSB). 2009. Holman Bible Publishers. Nashville, TN.

were nearby. He prayed, "Father in Heaven, I need all possible help to save him."

As he finished his prayer, all the guardians who were activated flew and stood next to him. They formed a large circle and extended their wings to create an extraordinary, unexpected, and sturdy featherbed. That was where Edward fell, on top of the angels' wings, in the same way a stuntman would jump onto a giant air mattress. Immediately after the fall, the angels lay him on the ground. Edward then stood up because his guardian angel had lifted him from the ground, and an enormous and sublime entity of light breathed air once more into his lungs. Edward started to cough, and then he looked to the people coming toward him, all in awe because he was alive.

Edward was awakened by his mother. "Time to get up. Your appointment is the first one of the day."

He smiled, feeling a profound peace. His Redeemer had saved him once more.

Chapter Four
THE NEW CRISIS

T he wind was brisk and a little chilly that morning. Nature had started to announce the dynamic flow of seasonal change, moving into early fall. Edward was sitting on one of the schoolyard benches, waiting for the bell to make the official call to enter the learning world. While he waited, he remembered the main events he'd endured over the last several months. The rollercoaster started with the explosive convulsion he had suffered at his old school last summer, just weeks before his sixth-grade graduation. That initial storm had rocked and changed his entire life. Once it had happened, it was determined that it had indeed been his second big episode of seizures. The first one, not as strong, had occurred the previous night at his house. That event was responsible for making him so clumsy that he managed to break glasses and turn over furniture.

Edward liked Dr. Contreras, his neurologist, well enough. He was very gentle and soft-spoken, and he seemed to own the knowledge related to his profession. The physician was a tall man, very slim, with very dark and well-groomed hair in a modern style. Edward's parents also liked him, and the treatment he prescribed seemed to be working. Dr. Contreras had advised Edward's parents to keep a close eye on him without limiting his usual activities. That approach did not seem to be any different from his routine lifestyle. He was in a new school, submerging himself in an adaptation process that seemed to take longer than expected. Middle school was harder than the elementary level, but it wasn't just the academic part. The psychological pressure was enormous, and the bullying demon was ten times bigger and heavier. Despite all that, Edward had decided he needed to conquer his fears and adjust to the new ways of middle school. It was an exciting and challenging prospect for him, but regardless of the way forward, something was amiss.

Edward continued to have his conversations with God about everything that surrounded his life. The most significant adjustment he was facing was taking a new medicine to keep the convulsions under control, a medicine he might have to take for life. That prospect scared him genuinely. He was concerned about how this new change would affect his future life. His parents were now monitoring everything he did, making sure his prescribed treatment was effective without new episodes in the horizon. For Wendy Rivers, that was an easy task to accomplish; she was used to it. Unfortunately, the situation was different for his father.

Edward's father had always been an excellent provider and loved his family dearly. However, his weakness of drinking alcohol had always been a burden and perhaps a threat to the family's happiness. Shortly after Edward's first storm had occurred, his father had stopped drinking altogether, and that deeply pleased him. Nevertheless, now that his condition seemed to be under control, his father had initiated his escapades again and tasted the poisoned nectar from hell. Ethan Rivers was a good man—hardworking, amicable, and an outstanding scholar. He was ten years older than Wendy Rivers, but they loved each other deeply, and the age difference had never been an issue. He was of average height, with black, wavy hair with salt and pepper touches all over. He had a stocky build, but he always conducted himself with the poise of a king. That feature was a significant element of his personality. Unfortunately, Edward never could see himself being that way.

18

Once the alcohol touched Ethan's inner being, a slow and treacherous transformation took place. This process usually happened at slow speed. However, upon completion, Ethan turned into a complete stranger. He would seem cheerful at first; nevertheless, as Edward's father sank into the poison's embrace, he would turn into a zombified version of himself. The result was a shadow of the excellent man Ethan had always been. He had never caused any harm to anyone, not physical anyway. Edward felt that his heart was ripped into a thousand pieces every time he saw his father in that state. It seemed very sad and perhaps ironic that his father's behavior only corrected when a member of the family was ill.

Sharing his thoughts with God, Edward suddenly heard His comforting and soothing voice inside of him. "Remember that even if your parents abandon you, I will always take care of you," God said. The youngster immediately felt a warmth and cozy feeling inside that calmed his troubled spirit completely— the peace of God. Shortly after his Creator's encouraging words, Edward felt a moment of dizziness and disconnection. He heard a guttural sound coming from his throat, but it was short-lived, like a vocalization exercise. Simultaneously, his hands started to move rhythmically, and he couldn't control them. The episode only lasted for a few seconds, but it left Edward puzzled and confused. He felt fine afterward, so he decided to keep silent and forget about it.

Several days later, Edward was in his English literature class when abruptly, another episode occurred. It actually happened a couple of times, and Mrs. Connor, his beloved English teacher, asked who was making disruptive sounds. Every time an episode happened, he just covered his mouth, although that was not an easy task. The events were short-lived, and they seemed to happen mostly during the morning time. Edward's classmates knew it was him making those noises. Most of them took it as a joke and preferred not to say anything to the teacher. Others were so mad at him that they had decided to stop talking to him altogether.

One day later that week, Edward was sitting at the bleachers in front of the basketball court, which happened to be an open court and part of the outdoor school field. He was there spending a free period with a group of friends when a new episode started, this time stronger and longer. Edward stood up, attempting to get away; however, his body didn't quite respond. He then stumbled over the front bleacher seat, falling down the last four steps. Everybody laughed, and he got away with minimal scratches.

His friend Carlos witnessed the entire event and instantly knew something was not quite right. "Edward, are you really okay?" he asked while Edward stood from his fall, amid the laughs of his classmates.

"I'm fine. I just stumbled with that step," Edward said, but he seemed unsteady and quite confused.

"I'm not sure about that. I truly think you should tell your parents or Mrs. Connor about this. I've been watching you, and it seems you're having these weird episodes you can't control. They might be related to what happened last year," said Carlos.

Edward turned around to face his friend with panic in his eyes. "Please don't say anything to anyone. I will deny it if you do. I don't want to go through this again. I'm fine. It's just my nerves."

With sadness in his eyes, Carlos said, "If you say so, but if this happens again and it seems like you could get hurt, I'll tell someone." And he walked away.

Carlos was a good friend. He had known Edward since they were together in the first grade. Thinking about it, he was probably Edward's only true friend. His mother was also a teacher, and she'd been college classmates with Edward's mother. They'd even worked together shortly after graduating. He was aware of Edward's ordeal last year at school. Their friend, Elvis, had told him everything about it, since he'd been absent at school that day.

Carlos was a delightful and comely youngster. Small for his age, very thin since he loved sports, he was extremely shy, which was a feature shared with Edward. He had become good friends with Edward mostly because he also suffered bullying and rejection from others. In his case, it was due to the color of his skin. Despite what the people in leadership positions try to make others believe, the curse of racism is still rampant at all levels of society. To discriminate against another human being just because he or she looks, feels, speaks, or believes differently than the aggressor is the worst kind of hatred. Unfortunately, this curse has been present in the world for eons. Even our Savior was a victim of it from His own people. Centuries later, the entire nation was oppressed, dispersed, and slaughtered several times throughout history. Regardless of that, that same nation will rise again stronger than before, fulfilling the ancient promise made by God to Abraham of lasting prosperity and number.

Carlos knew he had to do something for Edward. He was confident that something was very wrong, and his friend's health was in jeopardy. Why did Edward have to be so stubborn? When he acted like that, it really made Carlos furious. How could Carlos help his friend without crossing the line? He was so deeply submerged in his own thoughts that he almost crashed into Mrs. Connor.

She reached out her arms to stop him from running into her. "Carlos, are you okay?" she said. "You need to be more careful wandering around," she interjected while extending her arms to stop him from stumbling into her.

"I'm so sorry, ma'am. I got distracted with my own thoughts," he said after collecting himself.

"I think I know why you're acting like that. It's about Edward, isn't it?"

The youngster opened his eyes as big as he could. His watery eyes met the peaceful and tender sight of the beloved teacher. She was very tall, with a cheerful and calming nature. Her long, bony arms were always ready to embrace and transmit peace when someone was in need. Even when acting firmly, she was able to communicate the concept of love and friendship with her actions. All those features made her the favorite school-teacher and an angel on earth.

"What do you mean, Mrs. Connor?" Carlos said.

"I've been observing Edward for a while now. I can tell something is definitely going on. I've known him and his family for years now, and Edward is not a disruptive student, you know that very well. I also saw him from the faculty office when he fell on the bleachers, and I saw you talking with him. I have no idea what you two talked about, but I think it had to do with those episodes your friend has been having."

Chapter Five
THE EARTHLY ANGEL

The atmosphere over the school seemed reasonable for the season, but it was starting to feel heavy and asphyxiating in the spiritual realm. The guardian angel truly understood that a new attack was brewing, and the first stage of it was already causing unease to Edward's soul. The lad knew something was amiss with his health, but he was terrified to share his concerns. Edward opted to stay quiet, dismissing the obvious, which was raising his anxiety with each new episode. The heavenly creature was sure that the enemy of the souls had planted that ominous idea somehow. Even though Edward continued to speak to God quite frequently, he still needed to learn more about his options and how the prince of darkness operated. Such a process would take time to accomplish, and now Edward needed all God's support and guidance.

The angel noticed that the young man's episodes had become more frequent and more prolonged each time. He was afraid that at some point soon, a new attack would emerge in an effort to destroy Edward's spirit. Lucifer was knowledgeable that God had a fantastic plan for Edward's life. The evil prince was going to take advantage of every possible opportunity to delay or even stop the materialization of that plan. He knew that Edward had been instructed in the Word of God, and with each learned lesson, the enemy's treacherous plan was becoming harder to achieve. Edward was still trying to understand how to improve his relationship with God. Nevertheless, the enemy was determined to win battles before an immense spiritual armor built up in Edward's spirit.

The young lad was talking with his friends at the bleachers while he waited for his next class to start. Suddenly, he felt an odd change inside him. His guardian angel immediately noticed two abominable gargoyles emerging from thin air, and they proceeded to attack Edward's spirit. They had been inflicting small strikes against him for several weeks now. These attacks were almost imperceptible at first, and the intensity had steadily increased with time. They had the purpose of causing a colossal crisis in Edward's life, precipitating him into total collapse.

The crisis unfolded, and Edward fell down the bleachers without control. The guardian angel immediately charged against the demonic entities in the name of Christ. Once the banner of Jehovah Nissi was displayed, the creatures had to flee. The Holy Spirit was already there, soothing, healing, restoring, and taking all control. The sequence of spiritual events allowed the youngster to recover, stand up from his fall, and walk away unharmed. The angel felt grateful that this crisis was averted, but his inner instinct was alerting him that a major one was about to develop. The angelic entity observed Edward talking with his best friend, Carlos, and he also noticed Carlos' guardian securing every step he made. Right after that, he saw the arrival of an earthly angel, while Edward walked away toward his next destination — Mrs. Connor. The bright aura emanating from her benevolent and extraordinary spirit was indistinguishable. This lady was placed on earth by the Father Himself to touch, transform, assist, and bless every child she encountered on her path. The Holy Spirit had gifted her with an excellent and developed sense of discernment, which allowed her to reach out and help children more effectively. That was her lifelong ministry.

"Mrs. Connor, what episodes are you talking about?" Carlos said, with deep terror in his eyes.

"You know very well what I'm talking about, Carlos," she said with a firm but sweet, soothing voice. "Your friend is having new episodes that I think are related to what happened last year. Why is he remaining quiet about it?"

Carlos felt discovered, unable to make up any answers that wouldn't betray his best friend.

"Don't be that surprised," said Mrs. Connor, smiling. "Remember that Edward's mother is a good friend of mine, and according to her, he is doing very well."

Carlos had no choice. He had to share with her what he knew. "I think you're right. Edward has been having these episodes for several weeks now. He briefly dozes off while he makes weird vocal noises. At times, he also has automatic movement patterns." By the time he finished, Carlos was in tears. "Please don't tell him I told you. He'd never forgive me for that."

The old teacher looked at Carlos with maternal eyes. "You're an excellent friend, and believe me, you're doing the right thing. Don't be afraid. We all want to help Edward. I'll find a way to talk to him without involving you. Now you need to go to your next class. Go in peace. God is always in control."

Carlos felt an extraordinary relief hearing those words. He was clear it was the right thing to do, all right. The youngster hated to think that his best friend would despise him for that. However, even if Edward remained mad with him for a little while, that was preferable to seeing him suffer and struggle the way he was. He felt at peace, knowing that his action would ultimately help his friend. The young man went on to his next class, feeling comforted in knowing Edward would be taken care of. Carlos was able to see that even amid a nebulous and messy situation, God will intervene when we ask for His help. Our Savior will glorify Himself through our weak moments, proving He is the only true King. Nevertheless, he certainly knew that a new challenge was approaching.

Edward's protector immediately directed himself next to him with additional vigilance. He knew the recent attack was nothing compared with what might be booming on the horizon. At this point, it was not a question of if another attack would emerge, rather when it would happen. The young lad and his classmates headed to their English literature classroom, left their belongings, and went into the routine water-fountain break before class started. Edward kept his pen readily available in his shirt pocket to save time. The English literature class was held on the second floor of the building, with its hallways open to the exterior to allow the flow of natural air. The water fountain was located at the end of the hall, right in front of the staircase. The youngsters formed the usual line to take a drink of water. Most of them remained quiet or spoke in low, hushed tones, since classes were about to start nearby.

The spiritual environment abruptly changed around them, turning heavy and asphyxiating. Edward's heavenly guardian immediately took his position. That was when he saw the two enormous demons. As soon they emerged, Edward started to suffer an episode. His hand became tight, and he couldn't let go of his pen. His throat opened and began to emit a hollow, guttural sound, so loud that the other kids thought an alarm was activated. Once that happened, Edward's spirit started to feel constrained, trapped, suffocated. The feeling was the result of the demonic attack. The gargoyle-like demon was attempting to strangle the youngster spirit. The other one devised Jason standing in the line, and as done in the past, slipped wrong ideas into his mind. Jason always felt inclined to boldness and danger. He clearly liked to dare into dangerous and even forbidden activities no one else would attempt to try. That behavior caused the opening of spiritual doors that made him a perfect target for the devil to use.

"Hey, dweeb!" Jason started to scream, "Stop that show! You know I'm the only one allowed to play tricks around here."

Edward directed his eyes toward Jason's ominous stare. His angelic protector initiated his defensive counterattack in the name of Jesus to stop the harmful influence. The demons fled right that moment, but Jason was already commissioned with a different, unexpected action.

Jason became extremely upset. He didn't realize Edward was unable to control what was happening to him. At that precise moment, Edward was standing at the foot of the staircase to the first floor. Jason pushed him with all his strength. Being under the influence of an episode in progress, the youngster didn't realize how he cruised the stairs downhill. His body twisted several times above the steps without touching any of them. Simultaneously, his heavenly protector caught him in midair, letting him down safely at the first recess area below, with his hand grasping the handle rail. However, his legs lost all strength and support, making him fall face down. That event caused his chin to land on top of the pen he was carrying in his other hand, penetrating his skin.

Edward was not sure what was going on. When he opened his eyes with total control of his mind and body, he was staring at the concerned and tender eyes of his beloved teacher, Mrs. Connor.

"Edward, can you hear me, dear? Are you feeling okay?" asked the teacher with deep worry in her voice.

"Yes, ma'am, I think I'm okay now, but my face and legs hurt."

"That's nothing compared with what it could be," said one of his classmates. He didn't dare continue talking after the look given by Mrs. Connor. Edward felt and seem confused at his surroundings. He was lying on the comfortable sofa located at the back of the drama classroom. That location happened to be at the bottom of the stairs on the first floor.

"Edward, dear," said Mrs. Connor. "Somehow you almost felt from the second floor. You seemed to have been pushed by someone, but miraculously, you landed on your feet."

"Why is it a miracle? It's possible," said Edward.

"Do you remember any of it?" the teacher said.

Edward could not lie to this angel on earth. "No, ma'am, I don't."

"Of course, you were having another seizure. It seems your convulsions have returned. They look different this time. I believe they've been happening for a while, am I right?"

"Yes, ma'am. Maybe two or three weeks," Edward said. He felt miserable and ashamed. "I just thought they would go away. But I'm so tired of everything. I can't go on anymore."

Mrs. Connor looked at him in a tender and odd way. "Listen to me, son," she said with profound authority. "God will not allow anything to happen in your life to destroy you. The only one who seeks and wants to see you frustrated, defeated, and lost is the devil. The Lord Almighty wants you to be more than victorious.[5] However, you can't reach that goal on your own. You need to trust Him with all your heart and have faith He will deliver you and give you victory at all times. Your faith just needs to exist, as tiny as the smallest of the seeds, the mustard seed. And with that measure of faith, you will move mountains and conquer giants in His name," said the teacher, leaving all in awe.

Edward allowed salty currents to flow profusely, burning his ocular lakes as they flooded out their boundaries. Nevertheless, his tears were like an ointment on his heart and soul. He felt the comfort of a deep, restoring peace inside his aching heart.

A voice well known to him spoke to his heart very clearly, "Your earthly guardian is delivering my message. Remember, I am with you always, my son. Do not be afraid. I will always carry you on."

---

[5]   Romans 8:37. Holman Christian Standard Bible. 2009. Holman Bible Publishers. Nashville, TN.

Once his tears stopped flowing, Edward looked up at the face of the loving Mrs. Connor. "I'm ready. Let's call my parents. I will not let Satan destroy my life. I will fight with my God as my banner."

The angelic educator and heavenly guardian smiled, and the decree of war was confirmed.

Chapter Six
THE GOOD DOCTORS

The good doctor's face was grim and full of frustration. "Your son has developed new types of convulsions," Dr. Contreras said with all the caution and formality he could express. "I have started a new medication that, in addition to the one he is already taking, should help him. However, I think it's imperative I refer him to a neurologist with more knowledge and expertise than me."

There was a short time of deafening silence that seemed endless. Edward's parents' faces were aloof and full of uncertainty.

"Thank you for your honesty," said Wendy, trying to rein in her sobs. "We're grateful for the way you've treated our son. Who is the physician you're referring us to?"

"I'm referring you to Dr. Sampson-Lyon, the best neurologist in the state. He practices at the state capital." The statement was like an ice bath, halting everyone's heart, considering that the new physician was far away.

The trip back home was eerily quiet. Edward couldn't handle the torture any longer and decided to break the ice. "Is anyone going to say anything?" he muttered in a soft and sad voice.

"What do you mean, son?" Ethan Rivers asked, surprised.

"Well, about the new doctor. He's kind of far, isn't he?" said Edward, almost frightened, knowing how resistant his father was to going too far for medical care or anything at all.

"Son, let me tell you something. It does not matter how far, deep, expensive, or crazy the journey becomes. Whatever I need to do to find a cure for you, I will do it because you're my son, and I love you."

Edward just opened his eyes, astonished. His father was not a person who expressed his feelings openly like that. The action took the boy entirely by surprise, and he decided to stop worrying and trust in the Lord. God would place every element in the right place, and he would eventually recover from this ailment. He knew the road might be steep, but he needed to trust that God had the final word. He had never failed him yet, and Edward knew He would continue to watch over him.

His condition was slowly getting worse with time. Epilepsy was the name, and at the time of diagnosis, he was only showing one type of seizure. The initial presentation was controlled with just one medicine quickly enough. However, he slowly started to present episodic outbursts of guttural sounds (vocalizations) with automatic repetitive movements. Those events contributed to precipitate the fall he suffered at school on the staircase. The incident miraculously had not ended in a fatality, since he'd fallen, or more accurately, been pushed down the stairs. After careful assessment, Dr. Contreras determined that those episodes had started with small, brief absences or "staring spells." Unfortunately, nobody had picked up on those events, and they had evolved into the longer mechanical ones.

All the events that kept arising around Edward were squeezing him like a grape in the winepress. He felt his head was going to explode, and quite frankly, he wasn't sure he could take more of this. He also noted that the medicine he needed to take made it harder for him to communicate with his Creator. He thought things were getting under control, but they became worse for him. He remembered the day he'd been down the stairs while having one of those episodes. He had no idea how he'd survived that fall, but he knew something extraordinary had happened that day. He felt like something or perhaps someone had lifted him in plain air and landed him at the bottom of the stairs on his feet, unharmed. The only way he could explain such a wonder was to believe it was a miraculous intervention.

Now he had to be referred to a new doctor. He liked Dr. Contreras well enough and used to call him the good doctor, but something was amiss with him. He always looked professional, attentive, and supportive. However, every time he came to his office, Edward noted a deep sadness in his eyes. It was like something was missing in his life. Even his mother had noticed the same feature and commented about it several times. During the conversation that day, when Dr. Contreras said he needed to refer Edward to a new physician, there was something that sounded odd to Edward. He started to remember that part as he returned home: "I'm referring you to Dr. Sampson-Lyon, the best neurologist in the state. He practices at the state capital."

A big silence reigned for several minutes, and then Wendy Rivers finally muttered some words. "Thank you again for your efforts. I hope that God has guided you well, choosing the right person for us to go to at this time."

Dr. Contreras smiled, with a hint of sarcasm on his face, something Edward had never seen before. He said, bluntly, "With all due respect, Mrs. Rivers, I believe God has nothing to do with all of this. I'm dealing with medicine, science. If you want to believe that, it's fine, but my conclusions are reached by a scientific process and the evidence I can collect from the patient. I know what I learned from science, not from God."

At that time, they all left realizing that all this time, Edward's *good doctor* had lacked the joy of the Lord in his heart.

Edward would keep Dr. Contreras in his prayers, but he understood it was time to go somewhere else. Knowing his father was entirely in agreement and would not oppose the referral made him feel at ease. "God, help me through this ordeal. I want to get better and prepare myself to better serve you," Edward prayed silently.

The warm and comforting voice of his beloved Friend spoke to his heart. "Do not be afraid, my son. Did I not tell you that if you believe, you would see my Glory?[6] Do not focus on the events around you. Just trust me; I will always be with you." And the peace beyond understanding soothed his soul once more.

Two weeks later, Edward's condition remained the same, and it was time for the visit with the new physician. Traveling to the capital was always quite an adventure for the Rivers family and especially for Edward. His parents had been raised in a small town, the same as him. Even though Ethan and Wendy Rivers went to college in big cities, it wasn't their environment. The highways, the tall buildings, the big traffic jams, the crowds, everything was different and loud. Each time they took such a trip, it was a joyful and exciting trek since it was to visit extraordinary places or family members. Presently, the purpose of the trip was different; it was a saga for his life.

The Rivers family arrived at the building where Dr. Sampson-Lyon's office was located. The family had traveled well ahead of time to get an adequate place on the patient roster, since the new physician would see patients according to the time of arrival. The building housed residential units in addition to offices, which gave the area a cozy and inviting feeling. Edward felt at ease with that, thinking it was a sign that everything would go smoothly. He was quite tired, having had only four hours of sleep. The reason for that event was that the doctor's office had instructed his parents about a particular brain activity study to be completed on the same visit. Once the office opened, Edward had his test done, and afterward, he had to wait for the physician's arrival.

Edward examined his surroundings. Everything seemed tidy and well-organized, with exquisite good taste. However, there was something in that office that made him feel uneasy. He could not decipher what it was, sensing how his spirit became aware that something was not right in the spiritual realm. At

---

[6] John 11:40. Holman Christian Standard Bible. 2009. Holman Bible Publishers. Nashville, TN.

last, it was time to enter the new good doctor's office for the actual consult. What he saw in there gave Edward the answer his spirit was searching for. He was able to see the clinician's diplomas and accolades. Beside them, there were also some little figures and artwork that ogled back at him like they were alive. They seemed to be representations of the so-called saints or holy people, but they were not from biblical times. They were martyrs of the Christian faith, elevated to the level of gods.

Edward's parents didn't show any signs of distress. Finally, Dr. Sampson-Lyon came into the room. He was an older, more slender, taller man than Dr. Contreras. He was soft-spoken, distinguished, and impressive-looking. He was bald, except for the hair on his sideburns and lower jaw, where he showed an exquisitely trimmed silvery beard. He opted not to wear a lab coat at his office. Instead, he was wearing beautiful clothing, including a very peculiar dress shirt. It was a unique garment, made of pure linen. In reality, it had the appearance of a tunic, although not as long. It seemed to be made in one piece and made the doctor look regal.

Edward heard an indistinguishable voice inside his heart coming from the heavenly throne. "He is wearing a ceremonial robe. He is more than just a doctor."

The youngster's mind was almost frozen by a wave of unfolding panic. The same voice immediately calmed him. "Do not worry; remember to stay at guard but with peace. He cannot harm you because I am with you, and he knows that. He wants to help others; however, he uses the wrong guidance. Remember, I will always carry you on."

Edward realized this challenging journey was just getting started. He immediately understood the Holy Spirit was warning him that the new good doctor was involved in shady practices. He could not be precise at what level or extent. Nevertheless, God Himself had revealed to him that the new physician was working on the wrong side of the spiritual realm. In front of him was this new amazing and famous physician, according to the earthly realm. However, the good doctor was a minister of evil.

Chapter Seven

THE FATHER'S BURDEN

The Rivers family was waiting for the new physician's office to open. The guardian angel designated to watch over them was aware of the prominent evil presence at that office. He was not clear how this appointment had been allowed to happen. However, he was later reminded of human free will. Edward's parents had made the decision and put their hopes on a good outcome from it. God has always been a gentleman regarding personal decisions taken willingly. Even though He will show the right path through multiple ways, the Lord always respects the final option taken by men, even if it is the wrong one. Nevertheless, because of His infinite and pure love for humanity, He endures His presence among us to guide us, protect us, and advise us when needed.

Once the family entered the office after completion of the brain activity test, the heavenly creature remained on guard. That was a clear signal that the family was not alone. The Lord Almighty was with them. The angelic protector observed that the office had several niches at strategic places. They seemed like small altars dedicated to specific "deities" or "guide spirits," as the good doctor liked to call them in private. The environment was heavy with the spiritual burden, but a battle was not allowed to happen. God was in control, and His command had to be obeyed, even by the followers of darkness.

Once Dr. Sampson-Lyon entered the office to meet with the family and evaluate Edward, the guardian had a clearer picture. He was able to see the so-called guide spirits or demons standing next to the clinician.

The angel's next reaction was quick, blunt, and definitive. "In the name of Jesus of Nazareth, commander of the celestial armies of God, you will remain blind, mute, and deaf now and always. I rebuke you in Jesus's name!"

The demons had to flee, utterly unaware of any future occurrences or conversations at that place. The angelic protector realized then that the Holy Spirit had revealed to Edward the physician's role in the spiritual realm and how the heavenly peace beyond understanding had engulfed him entirely. God was really in control.

Edward was unsure of sharing the information revealed to him by the Holy Spirit. His parents were very impressed with the new specialist and felt he was going to have good outcomes. After all, Dr. Sampson-Lyon was well-renowned not only in the state but in the entire country. He explained his interpretation of the brain electrical activity test, stating that Edward was a challenging case. Still, he was confident he would be able to control the episodes. The doctor then proceeded to increase the current medication doses and added a third one. A new battle had just started.

Several weeks later, his episodes were somehow more sporadic and less dramatic. Still, the youngster seemed to be submerging into a strange stupor. The medication had sedative side effects and a tendency to slow down the body's metabolism, which Dr. Sampson-Lyon said were expected blessings in disguise. He also told them that these side effects were most likely temporary and that the body would adjust to the medicine until the convulsions were finally under control. Edward's parents were waiting patiently for a positive change. Three months into the new regimen, it became evident that Edward would not be able to continue attending school. His parents decided regretfully to withdraw him so they could take care of him at home.

Edward felt isolated, helpless, insignificant, and almost forsaken. How had all these things happened? He knew the journey was going to be difficult, as discussed with Mrs. Connor. Nevertheless, he felt he was losing his mind and all his vitality in the process. Edward's daily routine was flowing like an old-time black-and-white movie. Everything was confused, foggy, incoherent, almost dysfunctional. He felt he was slowly disconnecting from the outside world, unable to express what was constantly flowing inside his mind.

The only thing that kept Edward standing despite the crisis was the deep spiritual connection he'd already established with the Lord. His visits to any house of worship were limited because of his physical condition. Nevertheless, he continued to speak in his mind and heart with his Creator. Furthermore, he strongly felt the Holy Spirit strengthening him every time they communicated.

The voice of God kept resonating in his heart. "Do not be afraid. I am carrying you on." He felt that support very profoundly every time they had an appointment with Dr. Sampson-Lyon. The physician had always been very polite and professional. However, despite the fog caused by his medicine engulfing his mind, Edward felt the spiritual tension present in the atmosphere.

Edward knew Dr. Sampson-Lyon had all the best intentions and knowledge to help him, as the Holy Spirit pointed out. However, he was also convinced the doctor was never going to be successful. All Edward could do was wait and see the divine plan unfold. He remembered the scripture that speaks to our lives in times like this: "Be still and know that I am God."[7] He wished his parents had the same patience. He had listened to their discussion about the matter several times when

---

[7] Psalm 46:10a. King James Version. Public Domain.

they thought he was resting. Wendy Rivers was very hopeful, knowing Dr. Sampson-Lyon's fame and background, but Ethan Rivers was a different story.

Ethan had always found it challenging to remain calm in troubled times. Before he became a family man, he had been determined to live his life enjoying the present. Physically, he was a comely man, not too tall but with a fabulous presence and personality. He always approached life boldly, trying to hide the big baggage and burdens from his past. He was raised in a home that suffered a lot of turmoil and the frequent absence of a paternal figure. He'd witnessed innumerable instances where his beloved mother had cried herself to sleep for a husband who often chose a strange bed to spend the night. He was the only son among three older sisters, but unfortunately, he had lost two of them at a young age. Miriam had succumbed to a horrible infection that led to meningitis, he'd been told, since it had happened before he was born. She was his oldest sister but he'd never met her; perhaps that was the reason he couldn't feel any grief. Reina's was a completely different situation. She was a year older than him when she died, and they'd been very close.

Ethan used to live with his parents in a rural home next to a busy state road. The stretch of road in front of the property was a straight shot, which inevitably tempted riders to exceed their speed limit while cruising. That doomed afternoon, Reina and Ethan were playing volleyball in the yard while their mother watched from the front porch. Ethan wanted to show off, and he returned Reina's serve with a strong strike that sent the ball to the other side of the main road. Reina told her mother that she'd get it and crossed the road, grabbed the ball, and immediately started back. No one saw where the black car came from. Everything happened so fast; no one had a chance to react. The vehicle hit Reina, and from the impact, she was thrown almost forty to fifty feet. She landed on her head. She was killed instantly.

Ethan had never been able to forget those events. The images continued to emerge from time to time, as vivid as the day they'd happened. His mother had never recovered. She'd continued living, but she was never the same woman again. After those events, Ethan had just wanted to live his life day by day, trusting no one and believing in nothing. That was his motto until he met the woman who conquered his heart and saved him from wasting his life, the beloved Wendy Barnes.

That was the time Ethan started to believe and trust again. He decided to try faith once more, giving himself a new chance in life. He married Wendy and decided to change his ways, as hard as it could be. Now his eldest son was sick, and he couldn't do anything to make him better. His youngest son, Anthony, had been sickly since birth, but he recovered quickly, bouncing back from every situation. In Edward's case, everyone that had evaluated him had been useless, and he was losing his patience and his mind.

"We need to do something now," Ethan said to his wife. "All this new doctor is doing is giving Edward more and more drugs to cloud his mind."

"He's the best in the state," said Wendy. "Dr. Sampson-Lyon always said Edward's case was going to be challenging. He is really trying."

"Why are you defending him? Don't you agree that this treatment is not going anywhere? I can't stay quiet doing nothing when I see my son sinking into a fog that's consuming his mind. When are we going to demand results?"

Wendy shrugged her shoulders. "Well, on the last visit, he said he's planning to talk to us about that."

"When was that? I don't remember that," Ethan said.

"He spoke to me while you went ahead to take the prescription to the pharmacy. He said he was fully aware of our frustration and your lack of trust. The doctor wants to try new things that he'll discuss with us at the next appointment. That is if the medicine adjustments he made don't work as expected. I didn't tell you anything yet because I was hoping for a response. Obviously, that didn't happen, so when we go back in a couple of days, we'll find out about those plans."

"Really?" Ethan said. "We'll wait until then and see what he has to offer. I'm ready to do anything if it will help our son." He sounded almost desperate.

"Me too," Wendy said, for all the spiritual witnesses to hear.

Chapter Eight

THE NARD EMBRACE

W endy Rivers had always been a strong and stoic woman—hardworking, trustworthy, creative, and deeply dedicated to her family and students. She also considered herself a woman with a strong faith in God, at least she used to think that way. Her life had been plagued with multiple challenges and situations. Nevertheless, she had been able to overcome those obstacles with one practice—trusting fully in God's divine intervention, knowing He had delivered her in each instance.

Wendy had been raised in a remote rural community. Her father had to walk long distances to work and provide support to his family. She had three older brothers; however, one of them had succumbed as a child to an ominous infection. Her other two older brothers had proudly served in the military in Vietnam and Korea. They were the heroes of the family. She was only a simple woman, created to help others and bring children into this world after finding a suitable husband. Or maybe not. Wendy also had two sisters, one older and one younger. Yet, she was the only one close to her aging parents. That always seemed like her duty, her destiny.

She had always wanted to become a physician. She had the grades for it and the desire, but her father only made fun of her dreams. "Okay, your name will be Mrs. Doc now!" her father used to say so everyone could hear. "Hey, everyone, meet Mrs. Doc here, the new star of the family." Wendy knew her father didn't mean any harm, but those jabs hurt her in the deepest fiber of her soul. Realizing how complicated and arduous a medical career would be, she settled for her other passion, teaching, and became the best elementary school teacher in the county.

Wendy Barnes was grateful for what she'd been able to accomplish, despite the lack of support from her parents. She promised herself she wouldn't treat her future children that way. The young woman promised the Lord to support the endeavors and dreams of her children always, no matter how odd or complicated they seemed. She met her future husband when she was only a young graduate working at one of the city's leading elementary schools. Wendy was immediately warned about Ethan Rivers' past reputation with women. "You can't trust this guy; he's never serious with anyone," they'd say. "He wants to play around, never be serious about any relationships." Those were the warnings she'd always received about the young man.

Nevertheless, Wendy had a different view of things. Ethan had always conducted himself as a gentleman. He had even visited her at home as part of traditional, old-fashioned courtship. He was really in love and demonstrated that for all the world to see, abandoning his old days as a bachelor. They married and were profoundly blessed with two beautiful children, Edward and Anthony. However, the demon of alcoholism still lingered and came from time to time to torment and try to transform her beloved husband. Ethan was never violent or disruptive. He just fell into a coma-like stupor when he drank. All that stopped when Edward became ill.

The young lad's disease progressed in a way that completely took Ethan away from drinking or being out with old friends. He remained dedicated to his family and job duties, trying to stay on top of each new challenge or task related to Edward's wellbeing. Still, time continued its course inexorably, and Edward was not showing any signs of recovery. Indeed, he was submerging himself into a dangerous and deep stupor, very difficult to escape from.

The entire situation was closely related to the amount of medicine prescribed to Edward by Dr. Sampson-Lyon. Some of the medications were barely available in the country. In those cases, they had to be purchased from Mexico or the Dominican Republic. All that happened thanks to dear friends' help and disposition. Even so, no progress was observed in the horizon, just despair.

Wendy prayed every night. "Oh, Father in heaven, I am feeling desperate. Please touch my son; bring him back to me." She tried to lighten up the day for Edward, but she was witnessed how quickly he was losing his vitality and strength. It was like a candle slowly consumed by a flame. Edward was too lethargic to dress or even bathe on his own. It became Wendy's and Nana's task to fulfill all that. Some days were good; others were challenging, but overall, his progress was minimal.

Edward didn't have a lot of friends. Wendy only knew of one real friend, and that was Carlos. He used to live in the same neighborhood as them and checked on Edward quite often. Be that as it may, his parents got a divorce, so Carlos moved away with his mother and siblings to another state across the country, leaving Edward without any real friends. One day, three of his former classmates came to visit. They used to be part of the class student council, along with Edward. Wendy soon realized their visit was to gather information they could gossip about rather than out of real concern. They treated Edward as a mentally incapacitated person all along. They didn't realize he was able to see, hear, and understand what they were saying among themselves, even in hushed tones.

"Oh my gosh, the dweeb has become a useless retard!" one of Edward's classmates said.

"I know," said another. "I kind of feel sorry for him. But again, I really didn't care much for him. He was always such a nerd."

They kept their staged act, and after they were gone, Wendy found the drinks she served them untouched at the kitchen sink.

When she made a comment to Edward, he answered in a clear and coherent voice the reason why.

"They didn't want any juice, Mama," said Edward. "They were here just to see the freak show. They were making fun of me, thinking I couldn't hear them. Everybody just hates me! What did I ever do to them? I thought they were my friends."

Holding back tears of pain, Wendy just caressed her son's head and tried to find a reasonable explanation. "Oh, dear son! Please don't speak like that. If they were saying those things, they weren't your friends to begin with. They probably didn't know you that well. They do not know how amazing you are. Remember that people who love you and care for you will do it because of who you are, the same way our God loves us." She felt a strange peace, giving her strength and comfort as she spoke. "When you love someone, you don't focus on the physical aspects or what they can do for you. You focus on the essence of people, accepting them for who they are — no judgments, no criticisms, just love, real honest love. If they are doing something wrong, you tell them with love, but stay by their side when they need you." Wendy finished sharing her heart as tears rolled down her cheeks.

"Just like Jesus does for us?" her troubled son replied.

"Yes, just like Jesus," she said, and they embraced, crying together softly, surrounded by an astonishing floral scent.

That evening, Wendy Rivers surrendered herself to her Creator. Opening her heart and soul, she muttered, "Oh, God, help me walk through this horrible dark valley. I feel I am losing my son, my firstborn." She felt torrents of tears flowing from her eyes continuously until she ran dry. "I feel desperate, out of resources. I know You are with us; I can feel how You give me strength when I need it, but I feel I am losing my mind. Please help me, Lord!"

Suddenly, a delicious warmth embraced her, providing the comfort and peace that only the Holy Ghost can. Wendy felt a sweet calm, and unexpectedly, an exquisite aroma filled the room once more. It was some kind of flowery scent, and she was sure it wasn't roses or orchids or other common fragrant flowers. Instantly, the young mother remembered a Bible story about Mary of Bethany,[8] when she broke the alabaster flask to anoint Jesus and bathe His feet with her tears. "Nard perfume," she said. "Jesus, You are here right now." Wendy remained prostrate in front of her Deliverer. When she rose, she was confident she was ready for the next battle of this tenacious spiritual war.

---

[8] John 12:1-8. Holman Christian Standard Bible. 2009. Holman Bible Publishers, Nashville, TN.

Chapter Nine

A CALL OF WAR

T he Rivers family was once more at Dr. Sampson-Lyon's
office, waiting for his ultimate plan. Once he arrived at
the office, something felt different, amiss. Unlike at other times,
the doctor was profoundly serious, almost arrogant, when he
began to speak. "I wanted to talk with you about the next step
in Edward's care. I think I've exhausted all my resources to
effectively treat your son. I've done that even at the expense
of my reputation." He gave Ethan a reproachful look.

"What do you mean?" Ethan Rivers said, appalled. Wendy
remained speechless.

"What I mean, and with all due respect, is that I think you,
sir, have lost faith in my skill and abilities, and that is a problem.
However, I don't take that personally, and I want to give you
my personal opinion about your son's condition."

"Thank you for your honesty," said Wendy. "What is
that opinion?"

"I strongly believe Edward's condition has a spiritual cause.
I think he's being afflicted by evil spirits and that's why he's
not getting any better."

Ethan and Wendy were speechless and baffled. They
couldn't believe that a physician of Dr. Sampson-Lyon's stature
was saying those things. However, they could not speak against
it. Somehow, the surreal explanation the doctor gave almost
convinced them to pursue the matter. Edward was perplexed,

hearing his parents almost agree with the doctor's statement. The confusion came up not because of the declaration of a spiritual cause to his illness, which he accepted. Even so, it was the way the clinician recommended them to proceed. The esteemed neurologist suggested visiting a medium, "an expert on spiritual sciences," as he called it, to intervene and seek healing for the young lad. Edward knew that what the doctor proposed was against God's wishes. He also knew his parents were aware of that, but strangely, they considered the idea.

The guardian angel standing behind the Rivers family was wholly taken aback by the physician's proposal. The heavenly protector was able to keep the clinician's guide spirits out of the room. Still, he realized that the good doctor was brilliant indeed. He had presented his proposal so masterfully that he'd lured Edward's parents to strongly consider the visit to a spiritual adviser a real option. Additionally, Ethan Rivers had opened a big spiritual door and bound himself to it when he'd promised his son he would do anything to seek a cure. The spiritual connection, right or wrong, had facilitated the entire process in the spiritual realm. The celestial protector knew very well that if Edward's parents agreed to this, their free-willed decision had to be respected. The only option left to follow would be to pray and wait and protect the family as much as possible.

Once the appointment was over, the Rivers family decided to pay a visit to Wendy's older sister, who lived nearby. Edward always enjoyed visiting his Aunt Harriett and spending time with his cousins. Aunt Harriett was divorced and was raising her three children by herself. She had two daughters about Edward's age (one older, one a couple of years younger) and a younger son about Anthony's age. Even though they lived apart, they'd always remained close until the divorce happened. That event had occurred several years before the beginning of Edward's illness. Dianne, the eldest daughter, arrived first from school and was delighted to see her cousin visiting. As soon as she talked with him, she realized how fragile and sickly Edward had become. Dianne felt her heart was breaking into a million pieces. However, she'd learned through multiple instances how to handle this kind of challenge. Dianne decided to keep her feelings inside her and spend time with Edward, reading to him and just being there for him.

"Okay, Wendy," said Harriett when she'd gotten Edward's parents alone. "Now that Edward is with Dianne, tell me what's going on. Why does my nephew look worse each time I see him? I thought he was being treated by the best of the best in the state."

Wendy could not contain her tears. "I know. All he's done is go up and up on his medication dosages. This doctor also keeps adding more and more types of medicines. He still has episodes from time to time and is always in this stupor." She was now letting everything out. "I'm losing my son, and I don't know how to stop it!"

"Did he offer any options at all?" Harriett asked in a more comforting voice.

"Well, he has a theory that kind of makes sense," Wendy said with some reserve.

"What is it? Tell me." Harriett asked, full of interest.

"Well, he said the problem is probably spiritual in origin, and he's advising us to take him to an expert in spiritual sciences." Wendy paused. The only noise was the chatting Dianne made while she spoke with Edward in the other room.

Then, Aunt Harriett opened her mouth with an unexpected response. "I think that's exactly what needs to be done." Wendy and Ethan could not believe she was saying this. "As a matter of fact, I know the right place you can take him. I've been going there from time to time, as needed. We need to take him to Brother Frank's Temple."

Harriett Martin had always been a very outspoken and loud individual. Her demeanor and attitude let her keep going forward, regardless of the circumstances. She was Wendy's eldest sister, and she had always been hardheaded. Harriett had moved away to the capital due to disagreements with her father, probably because she was just like him. As far as Wendy remembered, she had always been a very religious and devoted person. Now they were finding out that Harriett had been visiting a spiritual adviser. "Don't look at me like that. I have to do it because my former husband used to engage in witchcraft activities. If it weren't for Brother Frank's help, I'd probably be committed or dead right now and my children lost forever. He was a God-sent blessing."

"No, it's okay," said Ethan in an almost nurturing way. "We're just surprised. It's a side of you we weren't aware of."

"Yes, sis, why did you never say anything?" said Wendy.

"And have Mama all over the place with sermons of how horrible and bad it is? I'm old enough to decide what to do and accept the consequences of my actions. You should do the same."

"Do you really think this Brother Frank might help Edward?" Ethan asked with deep curiosity.

"I think so. If Dr. Sampson-Lyon thinks this is the cause of all my nephew's ailments, Brother Frank will figure out what to do, God willing." She spoke in the most tender voice Wendy had ever heard from her, almost eerie.

"Then, it's settled," said Wendy. "We'll visit him at our earliest convenience."

The response was almost like an explosion in the spiritual realm. The heavenly creatures present at the residence were baffled by the decision. Nevertheless, they knew there was not a lot they could do against it. "Oh, no! This is going to make this process so much more difficult for Edward and everyone," the youngster's chief guardian angel said.

"Yes, I know. Still, you need to understand that we need to respect their free will. All we can do is be there for them and protect them in all instances possible." Suddenly, the two heavenly creatures heard a well-known, lovely voice. They fell to their knees while the voice came loud and clear from the celestial throne, directly from God. "You do not need to worry. The enemy is trying to attack their strength and faith. However, he cannot touch their hearts. That is what you need to protect at all times, their hearts and spirits." The order resonated in the heavenly guardians' minds like thunder. They looked at each other as they continued their surveillance of the Rivers' family surroundings. They knew a call of war had been made.

THE EVIL TEMPLE

The road toward the famous temple was lonely and ghostly. It was situated in a small coastal fishing village outside the capital metropolitan area. Most of the land they crossed seemed like abandoned agricultural projects, for the entire field now looked like wastelands, lacking housing or any signs of human life, full of all sorts of wild plants. After twenty minutes of desert-like panoramic views, they came across several occasional houses scattered on both sides of the road. Finally, they arrived at the small village of Atollville. The name referred to the word atoll, which are collections of coral reefs that form small isles or groups of islands. A coral reef is characterized to be full of life, beauty, and activity under the sea, but Atollville was utterly the opposite. The village activity was minimal, at least outside the humble houses. The Rivers family was coming into the village early on a Sunday morning; nevertheless, the streets were almost deserted. Following Aunt Harriet's directions, they finally arrived in an alley behind the main shorefront, where Brother Frank's Temple was located.

In reality, the temple consisted of three adjoining houses. The smaller buildings located on each side served as office space, supply rooms, and other individual services. The central house, bigger in size, was the main sanctuary. Standing at the front entrance, the family was able to have a glimpse of the sanctuary. There was a side door on the left side, just past the main gate connecting to some kind of office. The rest of the main building was filled up with several rows of chairs, looking like a regular house of worship. The front of the main hall was different, though. It had six separated flat concrete platforms, each about the height of a regular bed. They seemed to be there as a place for people to lay while spiritual work was done with them. At the front central area was a small pedestal with a microphone for the main speaker to use. Finally, there was a central door by the posterior wall connecting to the back of the building. At the top of the end and lateral walls was a large, sturdy wood shelf full of different items, jars with strange contents, necklaces, boxes, and other tokens left by "healed" or "delivered" individuals at Brother Frank's Temple.

Edward was still under the influence of his prescribed medications. Yet, as soon as they approached the building, he felt his spirit awaken and become alert. He knew a battle was about to emerge in the spiritual realm. The youngster was also aware that his spirit was not the only one at stake.

The guardian angels detected the oppressive and almost asphyxiating atmosphere surrounding the temple compound. Shortly after that, they were able to confirm the presence of many angelic beings assigned to the area. Those heavenly creatures were there to pursue the protection of several individuals, people like Edward, who had been brought there by loving family members. They were all there in a quest to find hope and healing. However, they were in the wrong place.

"There are so many. How is this possible?" one of the celestial protectors said.

"Well, things can be challenging on earth, as Jesus warned men that it could be," said the other angel sadly. "Unfortunately, not all human beings remember the second portion of that verse. It clearly states not to be afraid, because He conquered the world."[9]

---

[9] John 16:33. Holman Christian Standard Bible. 2009. Holman Bible Publishers. Nashville, TN.

"I can see that. They just need to keep in their hearts that the only way to the Father is through Jesus—nothing else works!" said the first protector.

"Agreed, but we need more laborers in the earth that can spread the message. Let's continue our duties so our protegees can become effective laborers."

"Yes, let's do it!"

The guardians positioned themselves next to the Rivers family, ready for any incident.

The family was instructed to go into one of the side houses, where several waiting rooms were located. They were greeted and registered as visitors, and after a short wait, they were taken to the office left of the main building entrance. The office was small and bare. The only furniture was a small desk and a chair for the interviewer and several chairs for the guests. Only Wendy, Ethan, and Edward were allowed to enter. Several minutes later, the back door of the office opened, and three men, all dressed in white linen, came into the room. The eldest man sat at the chair behind the desk, while the other two stood behind him. The man sitting at that chair was Brother Frank. He was a middle-aged man with round glasses with a small degree of tint at the lenses, which gave him a mysterious appearance. He had a serene face, always adorned by an enigmatic smile. Once he entered the room, he did not speak at all. Brother Frank sat in his chair and started to draw on a piece of white paper in front of him. The drawing consisted of one big circle enclosing five figures. Two of the pictures were bigger, representing adult people, and the other three looked like children.

Once he finished, he took a deep breath and started to speak. "You have three boys, right?" he said without preamble. It was just a blunt, unexpected question.

Wendy and Ethan looked at each other, confused. "No, sir," said Ethan. "We only have two boys. Edward, who is here with us, and Anthony, who's at home with his grandmother."

Brother Frank raised his hand, signaling Ethan not to speak any longer. "You were destined to have three boys. You only had two because you decided to stop. You may have your reasons, but the original plan was for you to have three." The air remained dense and almost asphyxiating.

Wendy's eyes were full of tears after listening to the seer's statement. "Ma'am, I'm not saying this to offend anyone. It's okay when we make plans. The fact is that we come to this earth with a spiritual plan already designed for us. Along the way, we tend to modify such plans due to our living experiences. That's all."

Wendy and Ethan heaved a sigh.

"I know you're here because your son is sick," said Brother Frank. "I know he's been haunted by evil ones. Things got worse because of the envy of a lot of people around him. We just need to pray."

Everyone in the room agreed. However, the direction of the prayer was not the same for each individual. The old crone looked Edward in the eye, trying to find something, establish some kind of connection. Be that as it may, that was not possible. He could not even touch the young lad. "Well, now is time for the service, and after that, you will take him upfront for the final prayer gathering," the seer said, trying to hide his frustration. "There is a tough battle going on. Your son is precious to both teams. We'll see who will win him." And with that statement, the expert in spiritual sciences stood up and left the room.

Wendy and Ethan were utterly perplexed. The revelation they'd been given was totally unexpected. Now they knew their son was a trophy in the spiritual realm. That information seemed too extreme to handle. Once they came out, Aunt Harriett wanted to know what had happened. Sobbing, Wendy was able to explain what she could.

"Wendy, I know you are upset," said Harriett. "But aren't we all targets for both teams? I think God wants to bring His children toward Him. Still, the enemy will try to stop that by all means possible. Edward is a special case. The Lord has given him certain abilities and talents we aren't even aware of yet, and the devil wants to stop the fulfillment of his destiny. I know it's difficult, but we need to fight for him."

The music for the service started. It was catchy and melodic, but the majority of the lyrics were chants Wendy and Ethan had never heard before. In between the chants, Brother Frank was just sharing how the work of "their spiritual aides" was able to provide healing and deliverance to several individuals in particular. Among those mentioned were former singers, local media celebrities, and even several state senators. He also denounced several well-known state politicians that, according to him, were involved in deep, dark witchcraft. Brother Frank made a statement suggesting they needed to be removed from office.

Wendy's mind started to fly away from her surroundings. She began to question herself for bringing her son to a place like this. Was she doing the right thing? If so, why did she feel so bad and almost guilty for exposing him to further harm? She then started to pray in her mind. "Oh, God! What I am doing here? Is this the right thing to do? Even Ethan couldn't handle staying inside this place. Please guide me. Protect my son from any harm."

The mother's prayer became an immediate executive order for the heavenly protectors. They both aligned next to Wendy and Edward while they waited for their turns, protecting them eagerly. There were several demons of different hierarchies roaming around, like noisy lions looking for prey to consume. As soon as they devised that the angelic creatures had been commissioned in the name of Jesus, they had to flee. Wendy and Edward were guided to a line formed in the space between the main shrine and the left, smaller, house. As they approached the front where the interventions were conducted, the atmosphere became more dense, signaling that the spiritual battle had become stronger.

Suddenly, while they were in line, a sweet voice brought Wendy back to reality. "Ma'am, do not worry—everything will be okay with your son," an old lady said.

"Thank you," Wendy said with a shy smile.

"You know, your son seems slow. How long has his mind been damaged?" the lady asked. It was an unexpected full slap to the face.

"I'm sorry, but his brain is not damaged, at least not yet. I will keep praying to God that it remains intact, as well as his heart, through this horrible ordeal." Tears rolled down Wendy's rosy cheeks as she spoke. The old lady smiled and said nothing else. After the speechless lady left them, they continued their walk toward the sacrifice pit.

Chapter Eleven
THE NICE LADY

The heavenly creatures kept their guard rigorously. They now had complete legal rights given by Wendy's plea to the heavens. Several demonic living beings were roaming around to attack and cause spiritual chaos but were unable to ever get close to Edward or his mother. Edward and Wendy continued forming a line on the left side of the main sanctuary. The area was an adjoined hallway between the big central house and the left-sided small property, where they had registered earlier. As they approached the frontal part of the main building where the altar and concrete platforms were located, the chanting and prayer were louder, almost unbearable at times.

Wendy's heart was pounding extremely fast. She felt like her chest would explode. Ethan had decided to wait outside, feeling overwhelmed. As they approached the front, Wendy thought she could not stay there any longer. However, the young mother kept having this premonition that moving away now would bring retaliation or an attack upon their family.

She felt a light pat on her shoulder. When she turned, she was ready to answer any adverse comments, thinking the old lady had decided to return. She was greeted by a completely different face. It was a lady about Wendy's age, showing the most beautiful smile she'd ever seen. She was tall and slender, had long auburn hair arranged in a ponytail, and expressive brown eyes, and her entire being emanated peace. The lady seemed entirely out of place; still, she was dressed in a linen uniform like the other ushers but with a brighter tone.

"Don't be afraid, Mrs. Rivers," the lady said in a low voice. "My name is Esther, and I will be accompanying Edward. No harm will come to him at all. I will remain next to your son at all times. The Father has sent me along with my allies to make certain of it." It was almost a whisper, yet Wendy heard it loud and clear. Wendy Rivers felt an overwhelming peace embracing her, and she was sure the nice lady was from *the good* team.

The line continued to move. The guardian angels noticed a unique visitor next to Edward and his mother. They were surprised since they were able to recognize that visitor. The angelic beings looked at each other with amazement, and, out of the blue, Esther looked at them with a most beautiful smile. They both immediately realized that one of their own, an angelic creature, was standing there with mother and son as an ally while they continued their guarding duties. The protectors realized that the Lord was working yet in mysterious and diverse ways. They also knew that the Creator had terrific plans with this family, particularly this child.

Wendy and Edward finally arrived at the back gate, and it was time for Edward to lay down on one of the concrete platforms. Wendy was told by one of the ushers that they would pray and intervene on her son's behalf to help him with his tribulations. Wendy noticed that the usher explaining the process to her was not the nice lady she had met several minutes ago.

Before the young mother was able to say anything, an almost angelical voice got her attention. When she turned to look, Wendy met Esther once more. "Don't worry, ma'am. I will be standing by Edward's side the entire time and will bring him safely back to you." Wendy immediately felt a wave of immense peace.

Edward was taken by the nice lady, and she noticed that no one else dared to approach them. The other ushers walked around Edward and Esther, not even touching or talking to them. It was like something or someone was surrounding them, shielding both from any harm. Wendy remembered the scripture that says that the Lord is a shield around us, our glory, and the one who lifts our head.[10] Wendy realized her son was accompanied by an exceptional person.

Edward walked beside Esther, and she helped him to climb into the small step and lie down on the concrete slab. The young lad started to feel uneasy once he lay down; however, the sweet voice of his beautiful companion gave him peace. "Don't be afraid. The Lord, our Shepherd, the King of Kings, is with you. No one can harm you or your family. Just keep the faith."

Once Edward heard that powerful confirmation, he felt at ease, bathed in peace, mercy, and grace. The youngster knew the Holy Spirit was there to protect him from any harm. He realized he was in the middle of the enemy camp, and despite that, he was under the shadow of the Almighty.

Edward remained on the concrete slab surrounded by indescribable peace. The ushers would come and go around his position, but they didn't dare touch him at all. Every time any individual tried to approach or lay hands on Edward, he was immediately repelled. Some of them even ran out and remained in a strange stupor. No one was harmed, but no one was allowed to touch Edward. Finally, Brother Frank himself came close, made an incomprehensible prayer, and told the ushers to get him out.

In the midst of all this, the young lad was listening to the most exquisite music he had ever heard. Edward was able to sense the regal presence of Jesus next to him. He opened his eyes and spotted a face full of light and wonder. The only thing clearly defined among the gleam was a majestic and beautiful smile. Edward closed his eyes again, resting. After several minutes, Esther called his name, waking him smoothly. Edward found himself at Brother Frank's temple again.

---

[10] Psalm 3:3. Holman Christian Standard Bible. 2009. Holman Bible Publishers, Nashville, TN.

Edward was helped to descend from the concrete platform. He was then brought back to his mother. The usher looked at Wendy, and in a frustrated and tired voice said, "We did everything in our power, but we can't help your son. We are very sorry, but it's beyond our abilities." The usher immediately turned around and left without waiting for a reply.

Wendy could not believe her ears. Before she could answer, Esther approached her, and with the sweetest voice ever, she spoke to the anguished mother. "The people in this place can't do anything because God has forbidden them to even touch your son. God is with him. God will heal and deliver him in His time. Yet remember that He will not share His glory with anyone. He is the true Almighty God." And with that statement, Wendy felt calmed and took her son with her.

At the entrance, Wendy approached one of the main ushers, asking for Esther to thank her for her kindness. The usher looked at Wendy like she was speaking a foreign language. "Ma'am, I'm so sorry, but I think you're mistaken. I'm the person in charge of assigning duties to our ushers, and I don't recognize the person you're describing. There's no one with that name in this facility and no one that fits the description you gave me. That person simply does not exist."

Wendy smiled and left. The young teacher concluded that her son had been accompanied by an angel of God. During their trip back home, the Rivers family analyzed what they'd lived that day. Every member agreed that God had provided supernatural protection against evil and unthinkable harm. The experience revealed to the entire family about the need to return under the wings of the Father.

Chapter Twelve
RETURNING HOME

The Rivers family went through an in-depth, introspective process after the Atollville experience. They soon realized the decision they'd made was not in the Lord's perfect will. However, our Creator, in His great mercy and love, had provided supernatural coverage and provision. Ethan and Wendy felt individual guilt in agreeing to pursue an activity that clearly was not condoned by the Lord's teachings. Simultaneously, it was overwhelming to experience how He had continued to extend His mantle of mercy and love, protecting their son's life from evil forces.

The family understood the need to reconnect with their congregation and especially with God. The entire process was necessary to allow complete healing to occur while they waited for a final miracle in Edward's life. "We must return to the church and let God work with our hearts and heal us," Wendy said to her husband, sharing her deepest thoughts.

"I know, but it is easier said than done, particularly after what happened. I feel people will look at us with regret, judging our actions," Ethan said.

"No, dear. We're not doing this for them. We need to do this for God and for us. God is the important person here. We go to the temple in obedience and adoration to Him. The people don't matter," Wendy said.

"Okay, Wendy, let's do it," Ethan agreed.

Once the decision had been made, a spiritual door of blessings and opportunities opened up for the Rivers' family. Ethan and Wendy decided not to bring Edward back to Dr. Sampson-Lyon's office. Instead, the young family started a search and was contemplating visiting a specialist in another state. The decision implied the possibility of moving and investing a significant amount of money. Yet, the Rivers had decided to endure any needed sacrifices to help their son in his medical ordeal. A friend had close relatives in New York City, and Ethan had some cousins living there as well. Both parties were helping to find the right specialist so an appointment could be made.

Edward's condition was about the same. The youngster was still taking his medications. Wendy made sure she had enough supply, at least for the next three months, until they could find a new neurologist. The young mother really did not want to return to the "witch doctor" again, as they'd started to call Dr. Sampson-Lyon.

Wendy decided to register along with her husband on an upcoming couples' retreat that the church was hosting. The young couple saw the retreat as a way to reinforce their faith and relationship. Nana had offered to watch the kids while they spent time at the event. They both felt it was necessary to rededicate their lives and marriage to the Lord. Ethan and Wendy wanted to have a time of close fellowship with God, while He completed the work already started on their lives and children. Wendy felt a warm and peaceful inner feeling that reassured her that God would deliver her son from his current affliction. They just needed to have faith and wait. The young mother was still unable to see the answer with her human eyes. Still, she was confident the response to her prayers was approved in the spiritual realm and would come to pass in His time.

The heavenly guardians were commenting among themselves about the way things were changing at the Rivers household. "It's impressive how the love of our Heavenly Father can influence people's lives," one of the angels said.

"Yes, that is the most effective way for people to embrace God's gifts. They need to receive God's touch, allowing Him to work in their lives," said the other.

"Absolutely. Every time another human being starts trying to do God's job, things can be adversely affected. I have seen that situation so many times! However, when God is allowed to take all the control, no matter how difficult the journey can be, our Father will always deliver us. The love of His Son Jesus will embrace us, and the influence of the Holy Spirit will complete the task the Father started."

Edward was observing with joy in his heart how his parents had decided to turn their paths back to God entirely. Edward's parents had never really walked away from Him. However, the decision to look for an answer in strange and ungodly places was something that had given the teenager deep sadness, worsening his condition. Once the family had initiated the road toward the Father once more, he felt closer to God, even when he was not able to attend services. Edward also felt his mind was more alert, as the curse of the medicine stupor was not afflicting him in the same way. However, Edward knew the enemy was still looking for the opportunity to attack. Everyone would have to remain alert and prepared to face any challenges together when the attacks unfolded. After all, the Word of God clearly stated that the enemy was already defeated. Satan is under the soles of our feet, crushed and conquered by the blood of the Lamb.

Wendy and Ethan attended the church's couples' retreat. During the event, they were able to re-dedicate their lives and marriage to God. The entire process was a deep, soul-healing session. Willingly, they were able to allow the Holy Ghost to cleanse and strengthen their spirits once more. The whole ordeal would serve as a preparation for the road they still had ahead as a family. Edward and Anthony deserved and required a united and complete family. They did not need human rags without direction. And the Rivers family was ready to take on that challenge again.

The weekend after his parents' encounter with Jesus, Edward was at home, sitting in the living room, meditating. He was grateful he could have a clearer mind for some hours. Wendy, Ethan, and Anthony were outside completing some needed garden and yard work. The television was on a random channel, and a well-known Christian news and interview program came on. Edward was mesmerized listening to the testimonies of diverse individuals on how God had healed and delivered them. With each story, Edward felt an urge inside him growing steadily. On the final segment of the broadcast, a very nice lady started to pray, and for some reason, Edward felt the need to bow his head and listen.

"The Lord is showing me a young lad," the lady said with a firm voice. "He's about thirteen to fourteen years of age. He is sitting alone in front of the television, wondering when he will be healed."

Edward felt exposed, like she was looking and talking straight to him.

"The Lord shows me that this young boy has been afflicted with a neurological illness for about three years now, most likely a seizure disorder. It seems that all the doctors are puzzled and unable to find a cure for his condition. The Lord says to you today: I am the way, the truth, and the life; no one can come to the Father but through me.[11] The Holy Spirit asks you that you put your hands on top of the TV and surrender your life again to Jesus. Repeat this prayer with me."

Edward was absolutely sure that his Creator was calling him. He stood up, fell to his knees in front of the TV, and touched the electronic device as instructed. The guardian angels surrounded him, covering Edward with their wings, while the youngster repeated each word of the prayer, rededicating his life to Jesus once more. "Now the Lord tells you that today your healing process has begun. He will open each door for you to

---

[11] John 14:6. Holman Christian Standard Bible. 2009. Holman Bible Publishers. Nashville, TN.

walk in and receive the complete healing you need and deserve. Just trust in Him. He is carrying you on." Edward knew when he rose from the floor that his Savior had given him the victory. And all that happened because the whole family had returned home to the Father.

Chapter Thirteen

THE PROMISED HEALING

Returning home to the open arms of the Father was a decision that entirely changed how the following events unfolded for the Rivers household. A permanent peace, reflected by the presence of divine protection sent by the living God, kept everyone energetic and hopeful. That was a reality, despite all odds against Edward's future. One day, Wendy was gathering documents and medical records copies in preparation for a potential trip to New York. The young mother was interrupted by a phone call that would change everything at once.

"Hello, Rivers residence, may I help you?" she said into the phone.

"Yes, Wendy, this is Clara Connor, Edward's teacher. How are you?" said the sweet-voiced teacher.

"Clara, what a nice surprise! We're fine. How are you?" said Wendy.

"I am doing well. Just counting the days since, as you know, I'm retiring soon."

"Yes, I heard. But someone told me you are taking another job."

"Well, kind of," Clara said. "My husband and I will become senior pastors of a church located upstate. I'll be working in ministry full time. That has been a dream for both of us and is finally happening. Anyway, I was calling about a different matter. Are you and Ethan still planning to go to New York?"

"Actually, yes, we're waiting for the appointment. It's challenging to get one quickly. Be that as it may, I hope the Lord will intervene in our favor."

"Well, dear, I truly believe that indeed, He has," said Clara. "My daughter, who works with the medical school in the capital, just told me that a new pediatric neurologist just opened his practice near them. This doctor completed his training with Harvard Medical School and has now decided to return to his home state. He's the first of his kind in the state. It's a God-sent blessing, Wendy."

The young teacher was utterly speechless, on her knees, crying. Her cry was not of sadness but of joy and gratitude. The Lord was providing the resources needed for His work to be fulfilled. When she finally was able to speak, she uttered a thank you in a whisper to her dear friend.

"Don't worry. Write down this information. My daughter already spoke with Dr. Valder-Blass, and the office is expecting your call to arrange an appointment. Oh, and before I forget, do you know the best part of all this?" Clara asked.

"No, Clara, what?"

"This doctor is a believer. His life and career have been committed to God. This is God's perfect plan. You'll see." And with that, the blessing was complete.

Edward was ultimately in awe when his parents shared the good news with him. Mrs. Connor continued to be the earthly angel in his life. The young lad couldn't comprehend how beautiful and profound the love of God was in his life. During his prayer time, he just showed his gratitude, recognizing the majesty and power of His Creator and praising His name. Edward also felt the love of God toward him, just a teenage boy loved by the Maker of heavens and earth all the same. "Oh God, how magnificent are Your works and wonders! I can only express my gratitude, surrendering my life to You. You are so good in my life! I know the journey is not over yet, but You have all the control and will provide for my needs as You will," Edward prayed.

Two weeks later, the Rivers family was on their way to the capital once more to visit the new physician. The doctor's first name was a confirmation of God's intervention. Emmanuel Valder-Blass was his full name. Emmanuel, which means "God with us," is one of the names of our Savior. They arrived very early, as they usually did in these cases, and made the first place in the waiting roster. The family was told to come prepared for a possible hospital stay, depending on the doctor's assessment. Edward never enjoyed those stays because they were associated with inadequate sleep for everyone and tons of tests. Nevertheless, the youngster knew that this time, things were different, all because deliverance was nearby.

Once the receptionist arrived and they entered the office, the family noted a totally different ambiance than in the previous doctor's office. Carolyn, Dr. Valder-Blass's receptionist, was a charming, petite, energetic young woman. Her skin was chocolate-brown, and she had the most beautiful curly hair Edward had ever seen in his life. The young lady always had a smile despite any circumstance around. Still, she had the right words for each situation. Despite being petite, she was a dynamo, full of energy and excitement, the perfect personality for the location, a brewing busy practice. Edward could sense how different the environment felt in his spirit. That situation was mostly due to the man leading the practice, who was a believer. The young lad also knew that the enemy was still looking for an opportunity to attack and cause havoc. Recognizing that reality was important for Edward. The named situation would drive everyone to remain alert and prepared to face any unexpected encounters. This is how they would be more than conquerors always.

Dr. Valder-Blass stepped into the office. He was a pleasant young man in his mid-thirties, tall, a little on the heavier side, but not too much. He had a very cheerful and friendly demeanor. He was also a delight to talk to and exchange diverse thoughts with. Dr. Valder-Blass reviewed all the medical charts delivered to the office from prior clinicians. He then proceeded to ask his own questions and was perplexed to find out the number of medications Edward was taking, along with the dosages. "Ma'am, I don't want to sound disrespectful, but are you sure those are the correct dosages? That sounds too much for your son's age and weight."

"Yes, Dr. Valder-Blass, I'm certain of it," said Wendy. "I know it's hard to believe. I have read the way those medications work and their side effects tons of times. Dr. Sampson-Lyon said he was doing it to promote control, and at that time, he was going to start tapering them down. However, that never happened. Instead, he sent us to see a medium."

Dr. Valder-Blass continued to review the copies of the submitted charts from the other physicians. He was able to corroborate that indeed, the medications and dosages were correct. The treatments were given as instructed by Edward's beloved mother. "I'm so sorry, Mrs. Rivers," he said with deep embarrassment. "I didn't want to upset or offend you in any way. I just found the document that confirms your history accurately."

"Oh no, no offense taken," said Wendy. "You just confirmed to me that you truly care for Edward's welfare. I agree with you that he is getting an excessive amount of medications. Believe me, there were times that I thought of not giving all of them, but I knew that would make things even worse. I couldn't do that with proper guidance."

"You're absolutely correct, Mrs. Rivers. We need to deescalate all these medications and find the ideal combination and dosages, with minimal side effects. Doing that will not be an easy task, and I cannot do it without proper monitoring. I'll have to admit Edward to the hospital right away. The studies that I have received here show a volcano of epilepsy. I have never seen anything like this in a child with a normal condition, meaning with no other abnormalities. It's uncommon."

Wendy and Ethan remained silent and looked at each other, hoping for a word, a revelation.

"Do not worry, Mr. and Mrs. Rivers. What I'm planning to do seems bold and drastic. However, it is necessary to reach a breakthrough for your son. I'm confident that by doing, as I explained, we can potentially make the proper dosage changes and eliminate unnecessary medications."

"Nevertheless, I want to quickly see his responses and act accordingly. The episodes may become stronger and more frequent at first; still, we will conquer them together. With God's help, we will take your son to the promised healing, reaching a normal life full of health and love."

"Okay, Dr. Valder-Blass, let's do it," Ethan said. For the first time since their trek had begun, Wendy and Ethan knew the road to redemption was clearly before them.

Chapter Fourteen

THE SPIRITUAL FATHER

The day was long and hectic with multiple forms to fill out, a wait for an available bed, completion of ordered tests, and so on. By midafternoon, Edward and his family had arrived at a room at the medical-surgical ward of the state children's hospital. Edward knew it was going to be a long and different night, since Dr. Valder-Blass was planning to make drastic changes to his treatment routine. The process was potentially risky but still done in a stepwise fashion to avoid an intense crisis.

The heavenly protectors arrived at Edward's hospital room and quickly surveyed the surroundings. The angels detected the presence of several demonic elements, ready to attack and precipitate trouble. The protectors positioned themselves in strategic posts while they chased away demons in the name of Jesus. The evil creatures had no choice but to go away.

The hospital was an old, six-story building. The institution was the only free-standing children's hospital in the state. The structure needed updating, but the staff provided outstanding services with a golden heart. Once the changes in his therapy started, Edward was able to feel more alert and coherent, since that had been the most prominent side effect. Nevertheless, the youngster knew that things would become chaotic before a definite improvement was confirmed.

Going into the evening hours, Edward started to have more frequent episodes, still of short duration. He had a study of electrical brain activity completed upon admission. However, Dr. Valder-Blass wanted to obtain a battery of multiple tests when more frequent episodes were occurring.

The young lad started to feel more anxious. The sensation of losing control was always a situation that made him make impulsive decisions. That behavioral pattern usually caused things to get worse for him. But not this time. Edward had elected to leave everything beyond his control in the hands of the Lord Jesus. He is the one who brings all the answers in the precise time and according to His perfect will.

The celestial protectors noted the sudden change in the spiritual atmosphere as Edward's treatment progressed. Despite the angels' initial precautions, new demonic entities arrived to attack and induce complications on the young lad. The angelic beings knew that these creatures could not touch Edward's heart, but they would try to cause as much devastation as possible. Be that as it may, the angels were witnesses of the fact that big and powerful rock walls were erected in the spiritual realm around Edward and his family along with the healthcare team working with him. The walls were impenetrable to the demonic creatures, and the angels were guarding the air above every human being in the room, along with an entire celestial battalion that arrived to assist them. The prayer of just men and women provoked the activation of such supernatural resources. That was the key given by our God to humanity to unlock the treasures from heaven. That was the key that provides believers with the final victory.

Wendy was feeling very tired when the first rays of the morning daybreak showed through the hospital windows, greeting the world with the arrival of a new day. Despite her lack of sleep, the young mother's heart was full of peace and hope. The night was one full of multiple tests, more frequent episodes, and several very dreadful moments. Still, Edward overcame them all without being harmed. The episodes were finally under control with stronger temporary medications and a new treatment plan with only two medicines had just begun. All the test results so far were within normal limits, except for the study of electrical brain activity, which still showed what Edward's doctor called "a volcano of epilepsy." Wendy was finally feeling hopeful and grateful, all at the same time.

The recovery process was slow but steady. By the time Edward was ready to go home, he was taking only two medications instead of more than ten, with dosing adjusted to effect. He was alert, interactive, and very close to being himself once again. He was still having very sporadic absences, but they seemed to be just occasional, and his physician was confident in achieving full control soon. Dr. Valder-Blass made some final adjustments to Edward's regimen and finally discharged him.

Edward was feeling like himself again. Summer was approaching, and Edward's frank recovery implied that his return to school the following fall was almost a reality. The last three years had been challenging and full of horrible moments. Nevertheless, despite all that, Edward felt the hand of his Creator, guiding and shepherding him. He knew it was still necessary to go through a specific fine-tuning process, and he was ready for it. The youngster was no longer afraid. Even if bad omens were spotted ahead, all Edward needed to do was to trust in Yeshua. He was his Deliverer and Savior. The Lord had never failed him yet, and He never would.

Edward's new treatment continued successfully for three months after the hospital ordeal. During that specified time frame, the youngster had no more seizure episodes at all. Edward was feeling better than ever, alert, coherent, and able to do things he loved, for a change.

The young lad had another study of electrical brain activity study before his next appointment with Dr. Valder-Blass. Edward knew how critical this study was since it would help decide if he was ready to return to school. He had been out of school for an entire year and wanted to go back and finish middle school and retake his life as a typical teenager. Edward hoped to return to school and finish that stage of his life and prepare for the future ahead.

The day of the appointment with his neurologist finally arrived. The morning was very sunny and hot, heralding the arrival of full-blown summer. However, the family had not made any major plans yet, awaiting the doctor's final word about Edward. The youngster had been without an episode for almost three months. He was active, alert, and ready to retake his life once again. Other than gaining some weight, a common side effect from one of the old medications he used to take, Edward felt terrific.

Once Dr. Valder-Blass arrived at the office where the Rivers family was patiently waiting, everyone knew all he had was good news. The physician was all smiles. He seemed to be surrounded by a special light, and the peace transmitted to everyone as he walked around was almost palpable. "I have the results of your latest study, Edward, and all I can say is that there is no earthly explanation for this,"

"What do you mean?" Wendy said with a shy smile.

"What I mean is that Edward's study of electrical activity is completely normal. There is not even residual abnormal activity, which can be seen in an epileptic patient while they recover. The study is completely normal."

The family was utterly ecstatic. "Does this mean our son is finally cured?" Ethan Rivers asked with tears in his eyes.

"Well, technically, we need to wait three years without episodes to certify a cure according to current guidelines. Be that as it may, if you ask me, I feel that's most likely the case. I think Edward is ready to return to school and live his life as normal as possible. With time, I'll taper down his medications until they're completely out of his system. In general, this is wonderful news."

Edward felt how God had removed a massive burden from his shoulders. He looked up to heaven like he was able to see the two big angelic protectors standing behind Dr. Valder-Blass desk. "Thank you," he whispered. The young lad then looked up even higher, to where his Savior was looking down at Him. "Thank you, Jesus," he said. Edward knew he was healed and delivered. He also knew he was retaking his life by the power of the blood of Jesus covering his life.

"Edward," Dr. Valder-Blass said.

"Yes, sir?" the teenager said.

"What do you want to do in the future?" said the doctor. "You'll go back now and finish middle school and eventually graduate from high school. Do you have any particular plans? Are you going to become a teacher like your parents?"

"Well, I definitely want to go to college. However, I don't want to become a teacher. I want to help other children like me to find the relief and cure they deserve and need. I want to become a doctor, like you. You really inspired me, and I want to follow your steps. Hope that's okay." Edward looked at the doctor coyly.

The doctor looked at the young man with tears flowing down his cheeks. All he could say was, "Oh, it's more than okay; it's an honor for me that you want to do that. Thank you. We need good lads like you. I'll pray for you." At that moment, a young man and a doctor became connected spiritually, like a father and son.

EPILOGUE

The return to school was not easy, since Edward was registered at his dad's school, and everyone and everything was new to him. There was a lot of bullying initially, but Edward decided to face the challenge boldly and didn't pay attention to any of the jokes or give in to any pressures. He often looked for opportunities to help the ones who were trying to hurt him, and through the process, he gained multiple allies and friends. Edward was not the same person any longer. The youngster realized that before he became sick, he'd been self-centered, wanting to get ahead in his studies and not helping others if possible. Now, all that had changed for good. Edward was still doing well in school. Yet, he also found joy in helping others, regardless of their social status, race, gender, or background.

Edward graduated middle school at the top of his class, being the only student on the honor roll that year. At first, he felt that honor was too much and didn't want anyone to make a big fuss about it. However, his own classmates didn't allow that to happen. The entire graduating class joined in celebrating how Edward had been able to overcome his illness and all his challenges, ending the race with a huge victory. His classmates praised him because of his decision to help others. In reality, the only one needing praise was the Lord Almighty, the one who had brought Edward to where he was standing now.

The years went by, and Edward graduated high school, again with honors. Everyone expected him to be in the front of the graduating class with the group he was assigned to be with during his time at high school. Nevertheless, he walked into the auditorium in the middle of the group with a dear friend. He decided to be with his sincere and truthful friends, rather than acquaintances assigned by obligation. Several years after graduating high school, Edward was finally off his medications and officially cured. He continued to glorify and give all honor and praise to his Savior for His divine intervention and healing. Our Lord Almighty was the only one responsible for his success and wellness. No other person, place, or thing was worthy of any praise or acknowledgment.

The young man finally graduated from college with honors and was accepted into several medical schools in the state. He completed his medical education supported by family, friends, and the living God who guided his life. The years of medical school were difficult and challenging. Nevertheless, Edward continued to walk forward, proclaiming the scripture that reads, "I can do all things through Christ, who strengthens me."[12] Graduation day from medical school finally came, full of joy and strong emotions. All the close family gathered to celebrate Edward's victory. He graduated with honors and an acceptance into the most prominent pediatric residency training program in the state. The residency program Edward was joining was in the same hospital he'd been a patient at about ten years earlier.

The family gathered at Aunt Harriett's house for a celebratory lunch, since she lived close to the location of the graduation ceremony. Everyone rejoiced and spent time together in fellowship. When Edward was finally alone in his room, he got down on his knees to speak with his Creator again. "Heavenly Father, thank You for all the wonderful things You have given me—my family, my friends, my health, my career, and the opportunity to help others. I owe all that to You. Walking under Your guidance has been the best decision I have ever made." Edward felt

---

[12] Philipians 4:13. Holman Christian Standard Bible. 2009. Holman Bible Publishers. Nashville, TN.

a well-known warmth and peace surrounding him. The room became filled once more with an exquisite nard essence aroma.

Suddenly, Edward heard the sweet voice of his Creator, "My beloved son, I am so pleased with the things you have accomplished. More than anything, I am happy and pleased with your walk toward Me. Remember—remain walking under My wings, and My blessings and treasures will be there for you always until I return."

Edward felt in awe, surrounded by wonder, mercy, and love. The young man realized once more how deep was the love of God toward him and all humanity. The Father in heaven had given the young lad the same key provided to Abraham, Isaac, Jacob, David, Salomon, and others. The named key is walking under the wings of our God and under the shadow of the Almighty always.

THE END

CPSIA information can be obtained
at www.ICGtesting.com
Printed in the USA
LVHW090725180820
663479LV00007B/493